What Hardy Found

Nov 20

For Mary—

I hope that you find this story compelling as it speaks with heart and soul. Thanks again for all your help with The One Great Story.

Grace and peace,

George Thompson

What Hardy Found

GEORGE B. THOMPSON JR.

RESOURCE *Publications* · Eugene, Oregon

WHAT HARDY FOUND

Resource Publications
An Imprint of Wipf and Stock Publishers
199 W. 8th Ave., Suite 3
Eugene, OR 97401

www.wipfandstock.com

PAPERBACK ISBN: 978-1-7252-7056-5
HARDCOVER ISBN: 978-1-7252-7057-2
EBOOK ISBN: 978-1-7252-7058-9

Manufactured in the U.S.A.   06/17/20

To the memory of my father, George, Sr. (1927–2019),
who, in his own quiet way, embodied humility, generosity,
hospitality, and a sense of fair play—values that
I hope all the Hardys of the world will embody, too;
and to my compassionate Beverly, whose enthusiasm and
encouragement made the telling of this story possible.

May all those who read this book discover something about
themselves, as they explore a bit of what it could mean to pursue
justice and well-being beyond the anguish of our nation's past.

Contents

Acknowledgments

THANKS GO TO PAT Smallwood and Brenda Hayes for reading an early draft of this story; to my daughter Victoria, who has read more novels than I have and knew when this one was not quite finished; to Professor Donna Gessell, who honored me with reading an early draft and providing expert feedback; and to my brother Carl, who revels in Hardy's outdoor curiosity and joy.

Prologue

"YEAH . . . OKAY . . . 'bye." She hung up the telephone and stood there, the way you might see a store mannequin from a side angle, almost reaching for something that isn't there.

By this time, her mother had wrapped a slightly tattered housecoat around herself and was sitting in one of the kitchen-table chairs. Covering a sudden yawn with her mouth, she looked over at her daughter. "What's he want *this* early?"

"He knows. Found the book last night and went back up there this mornin'."

"You seemed happy on the phone just now." The woman gazed at the tall child with a mildly quizzical expression.

Slowly easing into the faded upholstery chair next to the telephone, the girl let a long breath ooze out of her torso. "Feel like laughin' and cryin' at the same time."

Her mother tipped her head slightly, as a smile teased at the corners of her mouth. "How long you known?"

Wiping a tiny tear from one cheek, the young teen tried to sound casual. "Oh, I could feel it the first time we was up there."

"It be one of this county's biggest secrets."

"What?" The girl shot up out of the chair and looked at nothing in particular. Her mother got up, too, and clasped one of the girl's dangling hands.

"Baby, certain folks done run this town too long, and they's some things nobody supposed to talk about. We known it all—our people—a long time." She squeezed the girl's hand again. "But things gonna change someday."

Her daughter turned just then, and her mother could see the fire returning to her eyes. "Mama, what you talkin' 'bout?"

Smiling, the woman gently placed her hand on one of the girl's shoulders and rubbed it for a moment. "Great-gram's sleeping in the guest room. Go on, open her door a little. It almost be time for the stockin's."

1

Chapter 1

Moving Day

"Hardy! It's time to get moving."

He didn't want to look at his alarm clock, because he knew it was earlier than he wished it was. Saturdays were supposed to be for sleeping in, to make up for having to get up for school five days in a row. The only exception that Hardy liked to make was for an early soccer game, which happened only a few times during the season. Other than that—oh, and if he and his buddies had planned an outdoor adventure that required an early-morning launch—Hardy preferred to savor those few moments once a week, when the bed could feel like a silk pillow, and he was a prince who had no reason to rise from slumber.

"Hardy! Honey, let's go! I really need your help moving boxes." He knew that his mother always tried to sound friendly, even when she was in action mode. Expelling a long breath through his nose, Hardy paused and then began giggling to himself, imagining that he sounded like a young bull on the nature program that he had watched at school last week. Tossing back the covers with one arm, Hardy swung his feet out from the bed. He practically flipped himself onto the floor, stabbed his arm and index finger into the air, and exclaimed "olé" before he knew it.

"Honey, are you awake in there?" The voice was much closer now and sounded a bit puzzled. Hardy's face turned slightly pink as he quickly glanced around for the T-shirt he had been wearing last night.

"I'm fine, Mom, just getting dressed."

"Well, as soon as you can, come eat some breakfast. Jack will be here any minute with some of his construction crew to help us pack the truck. You need to bring out all of the boxes from your room."

"Be right there, Mom." Hardy was pulling on his jeans and had them just above his knees when his mother mentioned the boxes. Suddenly he froze—half-dressed, hair tousled, eyelids puffy—rubbing one side of his face in bewilderment. On the outside wall of his bedroom, he had stacked a bunch of boxes before he went to bed. They were filled with old toys, trinkets that older relatives had given him on special occasions, his favorite books (even the ones his mother read to him as a baby), all the clothes that she would let him fold instead of transporting on hangers, and a few odds and ends. The soccer balls, basketball, baseball glove, and the like were stuffed in a couple of worn duffel bags. Hardy stood there for a few moments, an almost comic expression on his face, his head rotating first one way and then the other.

It felt like his whole life was packed up in those boxes. In just a couple more hours, the only bedroom that he had ever known would be empty. With that thought, Hardy could feel his cheeks pinching up, his eyes squinting a little, and his lips quivering, but he didn't want to cry—twelve-year-old boys don't cry, especially when they are closing in on thirteen. "Now then, stiff upper lip," his grandfather used to say to him, when he fell off his tricycle and scraped his knee. But moving is different, Hardy was thinking. Moving could mess up my whole life! Shaking off his momentary daze, Hardy finally finished pulling up his jeans and then located some shoes under the edge of a packing box. "All because Mom thinks it would be 'fun' to live in the mountains!" he mumbled to no one.

After washing up, Hardy opened the bathroom door and could detect the unmistakable smell of oatmeal making its way down the hall. Oh well, he thought, at least she would let him improve it a little with raisins and brown sugar. She knew that he preferred his grandmother's breakfasts— eggs, bacon, grits, and toast. "Too much of that kind of diet," she would say to him, "will make you fat and dead before you know it!"

Jack was a family friend from church who had volunteered to help Alice and Hardy with the move. He had even offered to pick up the rental truck; that way, Hardy and his mom would have more time to pack the things that had to wait until the last minute. The boy's bowl of flavored oatmeal was almost cold, but just about finished, when Hardy heard the loud whine of a truck engine and a steady beeping sound just outside. Running out the back door and through the open but cluttered garage, he glanced over the fence, to make sure that Rusty was out of the way. The collie/shepherd mix had bounded out of his dog house and was standing on his hind feet, up against the inside of the fence, safe but still jubilantly greeting the big truck as it backed into the driveway.

"Mornin', son," Jack grinned as he slid out of the high truck seat. "Mornin', sir," Hardy replied, "just how big is this truck?"

"Twenty-six feet—why, you could almost play handball inside there, if you was one of them perfessers at the university."

"Mom says her boss likes to leave his office in the afternoon to go golfin'," Hardy said as he poked his head inside the cavern that soon would be filled with all of his and his mother's earthly possessions.

Jack snorted a little under his breath. "Golfin's for those with nothin' better to do." He waved a thick hand at the two younger men who got out of the truck's cab. "C'mon, fellers, let's git this pretty lady and her boy headin' on down the road."

Just then, Hardy heard the sound of tires rubbing against concrete curbing. He turned his head to see Jack's wife, Ruth, turning off their old Cadillac and then practically jump out of the front seat. "Here it comes," Hardy thought to himself, and he quickly shot one of those fake smiles up to his face before Miz Ruth finished gliding across the uneven lawn to greet him, as only she could greet her favorite young people.

When he was younger, Hardy would get hit with fleeting moments of terror when Miz Ruth would practically envelop him in her bosom and fleshy arms. He would feel like he was underwater and could not tell how far he was floundering from the surface. Now, he was used to her affectionate smotherings and took them in stride.

"Hardy, I am going to miss you!" At least, that's what he thought he heard Miz Ruth say during her first squeeze. These days, it was easier for him to tell what she was saying, since he had grown tall enough for his ears to get caught between her wiggly cheek and one or the other of her upper arms.

"Miss you, too, Miz Ruth," Hardy mumbled as he stretched his jaw back into place between the first hug and what certainly would be a second and longer one.

"What are we going to do without the two of you? Your mother is a special woman, young man, a very special woman. Don't you ever forget that now, you hear me?" The ever-smiling woman extended her arms and rested her hands on the tops of his shoulders, pausing for a twinkle or two, to look Hardy up and down. "Why, next time I see you, I suppose that you will be taller than me! Goodness sakes, time flies, doesn't it? Well, I suppose Mr. Haines and I will just have to drive up in the mountains one of these days to visit y'all."

"Yes'm, we would like that." Hardy's face was beginning to feel stiff from all of his polite smiling. Just as he was wondering how he was going to extricate himself from the jolly woman's attention, Miz Ruth patted him on the shoulders and then accosted his hand.

"Come now, Hardy, we shan't be any help to your mother standing out here in the yard!" Off they went—Hardy the marionette to Miz Ruth's oversized beach ball. Meeting them at the front door were Jack's two workers, hefting large boxes from the spare bedroom.

"Hardy, is your room ready to empty? Brush your teeth before you pack your bathroom things. Here, put them in this freezer bag and keep it with you, so you can find them tonight."

"Yes, ma'am, just a little more left to pack." As he walked into the bathroom and squeezed a dab of toothpaste onto his toothbrush, Hardy could feel heat under his eyelids, once again, as tears began to form. He stared out the bathroom window into the backyard, brushing absently and watching Rusty wag his tail as he barked at the men stacking boxes in the truck. One tear dropped into the sink, as he spit out the foamy paste, rinsed, and spit some more. Dumping the rest of his stuff from the medicine cabinet into the freezer bag, Hardy wiped the back of his hand across his face before leaving the bathroom and running down the hall to his room.

Hardy's mom had measured all of the rooms in the cabin where they were moving, to know which furniture and appliances would fit and which ones would stay. Those that stayed were replaced by smaller ones that she bought used from friends. Appliances, wardrobe boxes, kitchen boxes, toys, his mother's books and old LPs, lamps, the TV and stereo, cassettes, beds, sofa, rockers, desks, a few family antiques (the rest were going to other members of the family), kitchen table, chairs—it seemed to Hardy that there would not be enough room in the new house for all of those boxes and items! He had never seen a move before today, and he could not imagine where all of this stuff was coming from.

Jack and his small crew worked hard. They used a tall handcart to roll big items up the metal ramp attached to the back of the truck. Miz Ruth helped Alice clean, mop, vacuum, and chase down loose items, while Hardy took orders from anyone who gave them. After several minutes into the loading, Rusty gave up on the visitors and went back to his favorite spot under the slightly rusted swing set.

The renters had two small children, so Alice decided to leave the swing set for them. Rusty's doghouse would go, though. Alice's father had built it, with six-year-old Hardy's assistance. There was not much more in the yard left to take, even though Alice dug up a few of her favorite plants that could survive cooler mountain winters.

It did not take long for the late-summer morning heat to bring out the perspiration on everyone. Wiping his hand across the tip of his nose, Hardy wondered if he would sweat as much in the mountains. Today, his mother had filled a cooler with ice before the refrigerator was put on the truck, so there were refreshing drinks available all morning.

He tried to remember how it felt the last time he had stayed at the cabin. Rusty loved hiking there, chasing squirrels and exploring the hills and creeks that Hardy found not far from the cabin.

A honking pickup truck got Hardy's attention just as his appetite alarm went off. Out of the truck bed bounded more church friends, carrying plates of sandwiches, a tray of fresh vegetables (Hardy knew that his mother would want him to eat some of them!), bags of chips, and more cans of drinks. Everyone stopped for a few minutes, found some shade under the oak tree in the front yard, and ate. Alice did not sit still for long, jumping up from the shade and friendly conversation after a few minutes to walk through rooms that now echoed. Miz Ruth tried to keep up with her, holding a sandwich in one hand and a can of Coke in the other. A couple of the other women grabbed a bucket of soapy water and some rags and began rubbing down counters, window sills, and anything else that looked like it could use a little more sparkle.

Before much longer, the house felt, to Hardy, like a ghost of its former self. His room didn't feel like his anymore: it was bigger, boxy, almost gaping, and cleaner than he ever remembered it. In a few days, someone else would be living there, someone who would know nothing of what it had meant to Hardy.

When his mother told him that it was time to say goodbye, Hardy ran back into the house and down the hall one more time. Closing the door behind him, he stood in the center of his old room, where the end of his bed had rested, and gazed from one side of it to the other. He tried to take in the images and the memories that were flooding through his mind and heart at that moment, to put them into a special place deep inside of himself, where he never would forget them. One more time, he felt his throat tightening up. "Not this time," he said with his teeth clenched and his eyes squeezed shut, "not now!"

For a few moments, the boy stood in that position, like a statue. Then, Hardy's jaw gradually relaxed. He opened his eyes and looked around the room one more time. Hearing Alice's voice calling his name from the driveway, Hardy slowly turned toward the door. His lips moved with a whisper that even he could barely hear, "Thanks for everything." Opening the door for the last time, he ran down the hall, through the garage, and jumped into the passenger's side of his mother's used, but clean, two-door Maverick.

Rusty leaned forward from the back seat and began licking him behind the ear. Grinning, Hardy swung around to grab the big dog with one arm, but Rusty was butting him back with his head. "You big bag of bones!" By this time, Rusty was licking Hardy's head all over. They wrestled as best they could over the seats.

"So long, Jimmy Stearns School . . ." The one-story, flat-roofed, red-brick building was a ten-minute walk from Hardy's old house. In the car, the time passed rather quickly.

"You going to miss Jimmy Stearns?" Alice could see that Hardy had been lost in thought.

"No . . . well, maybe a little bit. My friends mostly. Hey, Mom, thanks for letting me have a sleepover with them before the move."

"Why, you are very welcome, my young man. Just because we are moving to the mountains doesn't mean that you can't keep up with your friends here." Alice looked remarkably relaxed, considering that all of mother and son's worldly belongings were traveling a few lengths behind them in a rental truck. She turned from her driving to glance at Hardy, just long enough to catch his gaze before looking back at the road in front of them. "And I owe you a 'thank you,' too."

Hardy's eyebrows shot up. He tipped his head down, as though he were looking over the top of reading glasses. Alice smiled as she caught his expression out of the corner of her eye. "Thank you for letting me fulfill one of my dreams." She reached over and squeezed Hardy's hand.

Hardy's brow furrowed, and his lips puckered. "Why are you thanking me? I'm just a kid. You don't need my permission to do anything."

Alice hesitated for just a moment. "That's true, I suppose, but I haven't thought about it that way." The trim, attractive woman paused again, this time longer. As she stared out the window, at nothing in particular, Hardy noticed her unusual expression, and his brow wrinkled up again. In the back of her mind, Alice always knew that the day would come when her son would want to know more details surrounding his early life but, until this conversation began, it had not occurred to her that this might be that moment. She simply had assumed that he would be too excited about his new future—living in the cabin that he adored—to be interested in his past. Now, she had a decision to make, and fast.

She turned to face her son once again. "Well, I guess I shouldn't worry that you are too young to understand."

Hardy felt one of those little chills that runs down the back of your neck when you are about to do something scary. Was there something about his father that he did not know yet—something too terrible for a twelve-year-old to hear? What secret had his mother been keeping from him? He did not want to appear nervous, so he tapped one foot to the music softly playing on the radio.

Alice saw the apprehension on Hardy's face. "Oh, honey, it's nothing earth-shattering." Hardy was looking out the window and realized that they now were driving by the university. He could barely make out the building near the middle of campus where his mother used to work, on the fourth floor, for Dr. Jefferson. She was still talking, "But I guess I've never said any of this to you this way before."

"What?"

Alice took a deep breath, as though readying herself to recite a long, memorized speech. "You know that your daddy and I grew up in Hanson-ville and graduated there."

"Uh-huh." This story did not seem to Hardy to be starting out too dramatically.

"And that he enlisted in the Marines, because he did not want to be drafted."

"Yeah, Grandfather told me that."

"Yes, your grandfather is very proud of your daddy. Well, he was shipped 'way out to California for training before he was sent to Vietnam, and I wanted to be with him. I didn't want to wait to see what would happen in Vietnam. I decided that I would rather be a widow than a broken-hearted girlfriend."

"So you eloped." Hardy was startled that he blurted out the next part of his mother's story, a detail that his grandfather had explained to him once, in the privacy of their "man-to-man" relationship.

Alice looked surprised, but they were nearing a turn onto a different road, so her countenance quickly returned to its usual controlled compo-sure. "That's right. We ran off together. It was not unusual back then, with all the free love and hippy stuff goin' at the time. Got married in Las Vegas, be-fore your daddy had to report to Camp Pendleton. Didn't tell anyone about it so your daddy wouldn't get in trouble—not even your grandparents—and my folks were very upset with me, as it was."

Hardy started to grin but decided the timing might be bad, so instead he commented off-handedly, "Yeah, I kinda figured you did something they didn't like."

Alice darted one of those knowing, parental looks at her son. "Well, you must know more than I give you credit for, my little man."

Hardy didn't know whether to grin or blush, so he went back to the unfinished story. "So how long were you in California before Daddy went to Vietnam?"

"Well, he had six months of training before he shipped out, but what you might not know is that I stayed there."

"You did?" For a boy whose world consisted of Draper and the university, Uncle Rufus's cabin in the mountains, and a few spots in between, this was big news! "So, was I born in California?"

"Yes, you were." Alice got quiet again for a few moments. Traffic was thinning out and buildings were getting smaller and smaller in the rearview mirror. "I know that your grandparents have led you to believe that you have spent your whole life in Draper but, yes, you were born in California. You and I lived there for a year, . . . until your daddy was killed." Alice stopped talking and looked over at her son in the seat next to her.

Hardy sat still and blinked a few times. He never had imagined that this might be part of his life. He always had seen himself as root-bound, a person of particular place. There was something about this revelation from his mother's story that shifted his psychological geography. He always had loved home, but now Hardy also felt like he was part of the bigger world, even if only in a tiny way. Sitting in their hand-me-down Maverick, as he and his mother wound their way—first on one road and then another—toward a new home, Hardy was not sure how to feel.

"I can understand that this might be a lot for you to . . . "

"But where did we live? We have no family in California. Did you get a job before I was born? Is California sunny and warm all the time? Were we close to the beach?" Hardy's curiosity began to take over his other concerns.

Alice smiled again, a bit relieved that her only child did not appear taken aback by this disclosure. "Ummm," she began slowly, "first, I boarded with an older couple in Encinitas. After a while, I met another 'secret' wife who was from the Bay Area . . . " Alice saw the blank look on Hardy's face and realized that he had no clear picture in his mind of the state in question. "California is a big, long state, Hardy. You must know that from social-studies class."

"Uh, huh." The boy was waiting to hear what his mother had to say next.

"Camp Pendleton is south, near San Diego, which is not too far from the border with Mexico, but the Bay is where San Francisco is, and that is about 500 miles north of Camp Pendleton. So, after your father shipped out, I went to live with my new friend and her family. They knew that you were on the way, and I did not want to move back here."

This next, almost casual, comment from his mother's story brought another twist to Hardy's picture of life as he knew it. Pausing a moment as if to soak it in, he asked without even realizing it, "Why not, Mama?"

Alice plowed on with a story that she had not expected to be sharing with her son this early in his life. She looked for the right words. "I wanted an adventure," she said. "I wanted to see more of the world. It was exciting to live somewhere very different, and I wasn't ready to go home. I thought that I could help to change the world, and I knew that my ideas would not get a warm reception here."

Hardy blinked again as he looked intently at his mother. "You mean, you did things like walking in those anti-war marches, even though my daddy was in Vietnam?"

It was Alice's turn to register a bit of surprise. "Well, I guess I haven't been paying enough attention to what your school books are saying these days. Have you talked in class about the protests?"

Her son ignored the question. "Mama, how could you be against the war when Daddy was in it? Did he know what you were doing?"

She decided to answer his last question first. "I never told him about the marches and the demonstrations." She paused, the way that people do when they are talking about something important to them that they have not ever put into words. "I didn't want him to . . . ," Alice paused, again, and then looked along the side of the narrow, paved road for a place to pull over. Hardy began to wonder what was going to happen next, but he kept quiet. When the car was sitting on a grassy spot away from the pavement, Alice turned off the engine. Hardy could not remember a time when his mother had acted like this. She looked at him hesitantly.

"Hardy, your father joined the Marines because he thought that he would have a better chance to choose what he would do. When the Selective Service did the draft lottery for his year, his number was sixty-one. He knew that he would be drafted. He wasn't sure what he believed about the war, but his daddy fought in World War II. He thought the draft dodgers were cowards, but waiting around to be drafted didn't seem right to him, either. A bunch of boys we knew from high school had already gone to Vietnam, and some of them never came back."

Hardy could not take his eyes off of his mother as she talked. Her face showed no emotion—she was somewhere else right then, deep in memories hidden almost from herself. This was a side of her that he never had seen. He didn't know what to make of it, but the boy was too curious to worry about that right now. Hardy could tell that she still had more to say.

Alice broke the spell when her head turned. She looked Hardy straight in the eye. "So, you see, honey, I couldn't tell your daddy that I thought the war was wrong. I heard things and saw things in California that I had never known or thought about. It was like the world was opening up and telling me to join in. We were young, so young. It was exciting, almost like getting drunk." She quickly stopped, her face flushing pink like Hardy never had seen. "Well, what I mean is, it felt so good to believe in something and take a stand for it. I loved your father, and I wanted him to come home safe but, for the first time in my life, I had something of mine that I could stand up for."

As though she had just unloaded the last large stone out of a heavy wheelbarrow, Hardy's petite mother turned back in her seat, facing the windshield, and sighed almost without a sound. Hardy felt like he was having an out-of-body experience—as though he were sitting in the back seat of the little car, looking forward at the two people up front, eavesdropping on stories and feelings that came from some unfamiliar place. He realized that his throat was dry from breathing through his mouth so, when he spoke next, his croaky voice startled him. He wasn't sure where the question came from: "So why did you come back here?"

"When I got word that your daddy had been killed, I had to contact your grandparents right away. I was a mess then. You were small. I was frantic. My friend and her parents would have let me stay with them, but I knew we had to have the funeral here, so I packed up the little we had. Everything happened so fast. The family paid for my plane ticket; you sat on my lap. We held your daddy's funeral, and then I started trying to put my life together again."

By this time, Alice had restarted the car, muttering something about staying ahead of Jack and the van, and they were back on the road. Hardy found himself staring out the window but not paying attention to anything. Alice was quiet for a moment, too, perhaps to allow her son some time to absorb everything that he had just heard. Suddenly, he swung around in his seat, looking at her again, only with a different expression on his face. "So this is like having another adventure . . . like California, right?"

Alice had been looking for the next road sign, but she grinned straight ahead as she heard Hardy's question. "Why, you are one insightful young man, Hardy Newkirk!" She paused again. "Leaving California was the other death that I went through. I loved it there, but your daddy was gone, and I had to take care of you. All of the family wanted us to stay here, so I did the practical thing—lots of kinfolk around to babysit you while I worked and then started college."

Hardy's eyes lit up. "So, when Uncle Rufus died last year, living in the cabin could be your next adventure. You don't have to take care of me like you used to, 'cuz I'm more grown up now." Hardy imagined that he had just put the last piece of a big puzzle in its place.

His mother chuckled. "In so many words, yes. And I decided that I did not want you to have to wait until you are out of school to have some adventure in your life. Sure, things will be different up here, but that's what makes it exciting! You and Rusty can find even more trails to explore. You'll make new friends." She paused briefly and spoke a little quieter, "and living up here will help you become a better person."

Alice's pep talk was getting Hardy worked up. He was smiling again, thinking about Cabin Creek and all the places that he and Rusty would go. Who knows what one might find out there among the hills and hollers?

Hardy felt his mother's hand on his shoulder, and he turned to look at her deliberately. "How are you feeling, son?" Her expression at that moment echoed far back into Hardy's memory, of rocking chairs and lullabies.

"I'm okay, Mama. Can't wait to get there." It was his turn to pause a moment. "How are you doin' with all this?"

Alice grinned for the first time since the conversation had started. She quickly squeezed his hand. "I'm doing great! Let's go see what the mountains have to offer!"

Hardy was feeling as though he had just found an unexpected treasure. Echoing his mother's sentiment, he shouted so loudly that it woke up Rusty in the back seat. "Let's go!"

Chapter 2

The Cabin

DURING THE LAST FEW minutes of their drive, Hardy and Alice didn't say much. Instead, they were greeted by vivid green hills, split-rail fences, winding curves, open pastures, and dogs chasing each other down dirt lanes. Before long, as they were leaving the hills behind and approaching mountain ranges and ridges, the landscape grew bigger, taller, and even more inviting. Hardy had ridden this route to the cabin a number of times in his life, but today he was noticing things that he had only glanced at absently before. Today was different, and he was beginning to realize that fact in yet another way.

Johnson Creek Road wiggled its way several miles off the state highway before leading to Shotgun Road, a section of an old toll road that the county had graveled years back but showed little mercy to clean cars that the occasional city slicker drove on it. Bearing to the left at any angle, and climbing a bit steeper than Johnson Creek Road, "the Shot"—as it was known to the locals—quickly gave Hardy and Alice the undeniable feeling that they definitely had left civilization. Dingy mobile homes sat shoehorned here and there in the hollers, invariably surrounded by rusting old pickup trucks that had not been roadworthy for years. Hardy began to recognize some of these places, mostly by the presence and condition of particular vehicles, even though he couldn't remember meeting anyone who lived there. Tiny, wooden structures with crescent moons on tall skinny doors played peek-a-boo with the little car as it drove along. Red-clay mud puddles and fingerprint smudges were just about everywhere.

Hardy's view of the mountains was now blocked, as Alice steered the Maverick off the Shot and onto the semblance of a roadway that was dirtier and even narrower. He had forgotten just how many twists and turns there were, how many times the roads on the way to Uncle Rufus's cabin went first up and then down, and how many times as a child he remembered feeling a little sick to his stomach by the time they finally pulled into the driveway. Still, his anticipation and a new kind of excitement were acting as Pepto-Bismol right then.

"I sure am glad that Jack is driving that moving truck," Alice declared, swinging the steering wheel right and left, hoping to avoid the deepest tire ruts and holes scattered in the bare red clay. She shot a glance at Hardy. "Remember where we are? Almost there!"

A few more spins of the steering wheel, and Hardy saw the bottom of the cabin's driveway. Uncle Rufus had dumped gravel on it every few years, so it gave the car a little better traction than on the bare dirt. To the right and up a gentle slope about sixty yards, the cabin came into full view.

Images from visits in years gone by began racing through Hardy's mind. Now he could imagine why Uncle Rufus had built his dream getaway on this spot. From the side of the hill, green, rounded mountain peaks rested regally in the distance, gracing the horizon with a peaceful presence. Close by on all sides, forests mixed with oak, poplar, and pine covered the hills and slopes. Rufus had situated the A-frame structure on the lot so that on winter days it received plenty of sunlight through the two sets of large windows, one above the other. "Passive solar gain," Hardy remembered Rufus saying about the design. Flat, dark-brown stones that Rufus had carefully selected and cemented sturdily onto the walls opposite the windows warmed under the winter sunlight and kept their heat into the evening. A woodstove sat next to one of the stone walls, its flat-black metal chimney reaching straight up through the steeply-angled ceiling. On colder nights, two sets of insulated shades could be pulled down over the windowed south wall, to help keep in the heat.

Even with these images of the cabin beginning to return to his mind, at that moment Hardy was still in the car, now bouncing every which way in its final ascent. Alice maneuvered it to the top of the driveway and then pulled to a stop. Turning off the engine and setting the parking brake, she turned to her son with a big smile and said, "Well, son, let's go open things up!" Rusty barked as Hardy stretched out of the passenger's seat, stood up on the gravel and clay, and stared at the A-frame structure. The dog was right behind him, bounding to the back door as if telling Hardy to hurry up. Alice had found the key and was inserting it into the lock.

As mother and son walked through the back door, with Rusty in the lead, Hardy became aware of something besides the old memories. Certainly, the layout of Uncle Rufus's cabin was familiar enough—kitchen to the left; bathroom, laundry, and closets to the right; with the large, open living room opposite, in front of the floor-to-ceiling windows. A staircase hugging an outside wall made its way to the upper section, complete with a small bedroom, storage space, and a railed loft overlooking the living room. Cedar planks on the wall sections without stones added to the cabin feel. A gable fan tucked under the A-frame above the top of the stairs drew cooler air from the windows below on summer nights.

Hardy readily recognized all of these features in this solid, modest cabin, yet being there now meant something altogether different. They were coming here, not for a visit, to live! The boy, who loved poking throughout the woods for whatever he and Rusty could find, had arrived in paradise. In his mind, Hardy was wearing his mud boots and cap, compass in a front pocket, walking stick in hand, happily wandering among trees and glades somewhere behind the cabin—Rusty barking, running, and digging with gusto. The excited boy had not even noticed the stale, stuffy feel of the air inside the place, until his mother had opened both front and back doors to let in a cross-breeze.

"Mmm, even on a hot day, this mountain air feels good!" Alice had closed her eyes, standing in the middle of the main floor, as a smile softened her face, still pink from the summer-day's drive. Her head was tilted up slightly, her hands open and turned away from her torso. When Hardy saw her in this pose, he blinked as if looking at a statue. For the first time, he thought he understood why she was so eager to move here.

Rusty's barking and sudden disappearance out the back door broke the moment's wonder. A whining sound from the morning intruded into Hardy's awareness. A split-second later, Alice jumped a little and followed Rusty. "Oh, dear," she almost muttered under her breath, "I hope Jack is not having trouble getting up the driveway!" Before he realized it, Hardy was standing next to his mother, by their car, peering down the driveway and listening for the rental van.

They did not have to wait long. The boxy truck's hood and cab jiggled into sight, and Hardy watched, with amazement, as Jack wangled the old beast around at the top of the driveway, to position the rear close to the cabin's front door. For the next few hours, boxes, furniture, and sweaty bodies crisscrossed the threshold, the floors, the staircase, and the rooms in a slow-motion blur. Alice played staff sergeant, Jack and his workers were the marching soldiers. Hardy took small boxes and other items from the man on the truck and tried to stay out of everyone else's way. He decided that this part was more fun than packing.

The truck was a cavern again, and the cabin began to look less like a storage barn and more like a cluttered domicile, when Hardy noticed another car pulling up on one side of the truck. About that time, he realized how hungry he was. As if an answer to his stomach's urging, more friends from their church in Draper piled out of the car, clutching paper bags and cardboard drink trays. Hardy was too happy to see the food to consider the long drive these friends had made to bring the moving crew some dinner. Alice appeared at the front door, blowing hair out of her face through one side of her mouth. Seeing the arrivals with their gifts, she exclaimed, "Oh, my! You didn't have to do that! Thank you so much! Hardy, Jack! Let's eat what Lola and Jimmie brought!"

Food always tastes better when one has been busy working, Hardy thought (and then he remembered this was something his grandfather used to say). No one else would care, but Hardy waited for his mother to tell him not to eat too many chips. "The sodium isn't good for you, and neither is the BHT or BTA." "Okay, Mama," Hardy replied through a bite of hamburger.

There was still daylight outside when the furniture had been arranged, both beds assembled, boxes placed in rooms to be unpacked, the well pump checked out, electric switches and outlets tested, and the kitchen essentials set up. "Mama, Rusty and I would like to sleep in sleeping bags tonight, in the living room."

"I don't see why not. But let's help our helpers finish up and say thank you to them before they leave," his mother answered from the kitchen.

"Sure thing," the boy replied, looking around to see what else Jack was putting together. Just a few more unpacking chores, and Alice told Jack that she and Hardy could handle the rest later. Always gracious, she thanked each person with a word and a hug. Hardy enjoyed the adult feel of shaking hands and politely saying, "Thank you for all of your help today," even though the women were teary by then and kissed him on the cheek anyway. Simultaneous exchanges of "Y'all take care now!" and "Come back and see us sometime!" filled the air, as Alice began to wipe her eyes. In another minute, Alice and Hardy stood alone, the whining truck sounds fading down the dirt road. Then Hardy realized that the sun had moved below the tree line and the cabin sat in the shade of early evening.

Alice put her arm around Hardy and pulled him to her side. Turning slightly, she kissed him on top of the head. In the dim light, as her arm remained wrapped around Hardy's back, he smiled the way you do when you don't know whether to act as though you like or don't like what just happened (no one else was around, anyway).

Venus shone in the sky, as Alice gazed up to the darkening blue-gray expanse above them. "Well, son, here we are!"

Hardy noticed that he was almost as tall as his mother. "Yeah, here we are." He paused. "I think I'm gonna like it here."

Alice turned to look at him through the fading light. "I hope so, Hardy. I sure want you to like it." He could not see the flicker of worry across her face just then.

Hardy tipped back and away to look at Alice's face, so she dropped her arm. "Mama, I can't wait to take Rusty out in the forest. We're gonna learn where everything is—the creeks, the trails—heck, we might even find some old stuff that nobody else knows about!"

Alice smiled at her inquisitive son. "Well, as long as you don't run into any moonshine stills, I guess you'll be okay out there."

Hardy looked puzzled. "Oh, Mama, nobody makes moonshine anymore."

His mother's smile changed. "Hmm, I guess Uncle Rufus didn't tell you as many stories as I thought he had." She turned and began walking toward the cabin. "Come on, son. It's been a long day. You get out your sleeping bag, and let's both hit the hay. Tomorrow we both have to check out our new schools!"

Hardy ran by his mother, but not before she tousled his hair with her hand. He bounded up the staircase to his new bedroom, dug around boxes and fresh piles to uncover his sleeping bag and mat, and ran back downstairs, Rusty barking behind him. His overnight setup was ready in moments, but before he could run back upstairs for his pajamas, he heard his mother's slightly garbled voice from the bathroom. "I'm brushing my teeth now. Come brush yours before you forget." Rolling his eyes, Hardy found the plastic bag from the morning packing and dutifully exercised his dental hygiene for the night. He and Rusty were snug on the floor, gazing out the windows at the stars, when Alice left the bathroom for her bedroom.

"Sweet dreams, honey, and don't look out at the stars too long."

"No, Mama, 'night."

HARDY FELL ASLEEP so quickly that he never noticed that his mother had opened windows downstairs and switched on the gable fan. Its hum was soothing and, after a few minutes, almost undetectable to the ear. The night passed quickly and quietly. When a soft shaft of morning sunlight reflected off a strip of metal on the back of a chair and shot across his eyes, Hardy began to blink slowly. Turning his head left and then right, he realized that

Rusty was not lying next to him anymore. The faithful canine barked from the kitchen when he saw Hardy's head move. When Hardy saw his patient, but eager, companion sitting next to his empty food dish, he jumped out of his sleeping bag and went into the kitchen to look for Rusty's food.

Rusty was happily chewing, following an exchange of rubs behind the ears and licks on the face, when Hardy turned back toward the living room and felt a moment of panic. He had not noticed that the kitchen door was open. Had he seen or heard his mother yet that morning? Without thinking, the frightened boy ran out the door, still wearing his pajamas (something he never would have done at home in Draper). "Mama, Mama!" This childhood address for his mother would have felt embarrassing under other circumstances, but Hardy was not thinking about that right now. He and his mother had just moved to the mountains, and she was nowhere to be seen.

"Mama, Mama!" It was hard to tell how much time was going by as Hardy ran past the car, his heart speeding up as he scanned the front yard and tried to think where he should look next. Out of the corner of one eye, he detected movement from a partially cleared spot on one side of the house. In a moment, he was running toward that place and then, in the very next moment, relief swept over him and washed away his fear.

Alice was sitting on an old swing, made of two ropes and a flat piece of oak that Rufus had hand-planed years ago. Her eyes opened as she felt the ground vibrating from Hardy's rapidly moving feet. "Honey, what's wrong?" The words left her mouth even before the meditative expression that had been on her face changed to concern.

Hardy stopped dead in his tracks and tried to slow his panting. "I . . . I didn't know where you were."

His mother jumped off the swing and walked quickly to her son. "I'm sorry you were scared! I came out here to the old swing just before the sun came up, to sit and enjoy the early-morning light."

Trying to regain his composure quickly—and not feel as though he had been silly about the whole thing—Hardy stumbled over pieces of words that were coming out all garbled up. "I wasn't . . . you weren't . . . Rusty . . . the door . . . " By that time, Alice was standing next to him and wrapped her arms around his shoulders, pulling his head next to her cheek.

"Baby, I'm so sorry! I didn't mean to startle you! I woke up early and remembered how much I liked sitting on this swing with you when you were little. We would play patty-cake as we rocked back and forth. Remember?"

Hardy's cheeks had turned red, and he mumbled like he did the time he forgot some of his lines in the Christmas play. "I remember this swing, and I remember sitting here on your lap."

"Well, anyway," Alice spoke absently as she looked into Hardy's face. "You are my guy, and I would never do anything to hurt you or frighten you."

"I know, Mama," her son replied, "but it's our first day here."

"It sure is!" Alice smiled. "We have a lot to do in town today, so let's see what we can rustle up for breakfast and then head back down the road."

As they walked back to the house, Hardy asked, "Can Rusty stay outside while we're gone?"

"Not yet. Let's wait 'til the two of you get used to being up here for a while. If he gets lost, no one will know where he belongs."

"Okay. Let's get our errands done, 'cuz Rusty and I don't have much time left for exploring before school starts."

Alice chuckled. "You are a Newkirk, that's for sure! We might have to build a cabinet or something next to the woodshed, for all the things you find that are too big or too dirty to keep in the house."

Hardy grinned. He knew that he had the best mom in the world.

Chapter 3

Pine Gap School

"I WONDER HOW MANY neighbors would have to petition the county before it would put some asphalt on this road?"

Hardy was wondering something similar, as Alice steered their beleaguered vehicle down the pitted and creased "Shot" and back onto Johnson Creek Road. No wonder there were so many pickup trucks on the roads out here, he thought.

"Maybe we should trade this thing in for a small pickup, Hardy. They can take the bumps better. What do you think?"

His eyes widened for a moment, as he wondered how the two of them could have been so close to the same mental wavelength. "Well, I never really thought about it before, but it might be a good idea." His own spoken words gave Hardy yet another thought. He swung around in his seat to look at Alice, as if to ensure that his mother would realize how serious he was, "What if the pickup had a canopy on it, for Rusty? Plus, we could use it for camping!"

"Now you're talkin'! But, first, we'd better see what is available and how things go with my new paycheck. I like the way you're thinkin', though." Alice smiled once again at Hardy, who was struck by how relaxed she had been through this moving process. He remembered how proud he was at her college graduation last spring, after all the years of working at her job on campus, of taking classes, of studying every night after dinner, and of helping him with his own homework. Not all of his friends' parents seemed as determined as his mother was. Whenever one of them would ask her why she was not married again, she would laugh and say something like, "I have my work, my church, my studies, and Hardy—no time left for a man!" Her friends would laugh but, to Hardy, they did not appear very convinced.

The car suddenly felt quiet again, and Hardy noticed that they were back on pavement. From Johnson Creek Road, heading toward Pine Gap, it was just a few miles the other direction from Draper on the state highway. When they passed a sign that read, "Pine Gap, 2 miles," Alice glanced over at her son, who was looking out the window at hills, hollers, and small patches of farmland. She had worried a little that this move to a much smaller town would create more of an adjustment for Hardy than he realized. Certainly, Draper was no metropolis, but the state university gave it something of a cosmopolitan flair. Assuming they stayed that long, would the county high school challenge him enough academically for college prep? Would Hardy feel that Pine Gap offered him good experiences? How will he get ready for life as an adult, the way that Alice felt her time in California helped her? Alice could not imagine that his tromping around in the woods with Rusty would be sufficient.

"All in a day's mothering, I guess," Alice mused silently, as the Pine Gap town-limit sign approached. This time aloud, she spoke in a tour guide's voice, "Now entering the community of Pine Gap—first stop: the school district offices." Hardy smiled, but then a flashback to yesterday morning in his old bedroom pulled the sides of his mouth down a little. Alice saw the slight change in his expression and tried a little harder to sound enthusiastic. "Time to get you registered and me assigned my keys!"

Alice felt fortunate that Pine Gap Community High School had advertised a position in art and art appreciation the same semester that she was completing her degree. Since the subject was not very popular, the superintendent had told her to be prepared to teach a section or so of English, too. It all would suit Alice fine. She believed that it was important for kids everywhere to grow up learning how to express themselves and be creative. She knew from her years at the college, however, not to be too eager to prove herself, as a brand-new teacher. Her boss, Dr. Jefferson, had counseled many students about the benefit of getting to be known and trusted by the parents and other teachers, so she was ready to work hard at her first teaching job but knew to "keep her head up," too. Her primary energy, she had decided, would go into making a home out of the cabin and helping Hardy enjoy his new life.

Mother and son had moved from Draper to Pine Gap with enough time to unpack most of their boxes before Alice had to report for teacher days at the high school. Here at the district office, she signed final paperwork and filled out the necessary forms for Hardy to be enrolled, then they returned to the car and drove to Hardy's new school. He was too focused on seeing it to notice anything about the town as they drove the streets. A school secretary greeted them at the building's front door and introduced Alice and Hardy to the principal, who reviewed Hardy's school records and assigned him to classes and teachers. When they were leaving, the principal stuck out his hand for Hardy to shake and said, "You're in middle school, son. Welcome to Pine Gap!"

"Thank you, sir," Hardy replied, trying to sound grown up in front of his mother and new principal. Alice's school building was a few minutes' drive in another direction. Now Hardy began to notice buildings, streets, houses, people, and other things about the town of Pine Gap. Its courthouse was smaller than the one in Draper, but it looked very similar: a red-brick, almost cube-shaped structure that had been built a century ago and was showing some deferred maintenance. Still, it looked rather stately, sitting in the middle of town, with streets and commercial buildings on all sides. Glancing from the car, Hardy thought that some of them looked abandoned and others could have used some fresh paint on their signs and wood facades. It was another hot day, but adults and children were walking the sidewalks, getting in and out of automobiles, and going in and out of stores and offices. It isn't Draper, Hardy thought, but that's alright. I've got plenty of hills and streams to explore around our cabin. Then he giggled to himself as he realized that he already was thinking of the new home as theirs.

At the high school, Hardy helped Alice go through all the materials and supplies in the art room, so that she could decide what her budget would allow her to order. He had grown up with easels, brushes, weaving frames, fabrics, and other art supplies scattered in a pleasantly chaotic manner across the floor, walls, and containers in their spare bedroom. As she sorted through things in the art room, Alice had that look on her face that Hardy had seen many times when she was studying at home. Once she had a good look at what was there, she took a deep breath, scrutinized the rest of the room again, and exhaled, "Well, this is not an art academy, but we will make it work!"

A stop at Pine Gap's largest grocery store took about an hour since they were stocking the kitchen with things that they did not bring from Draper. Alice would give Hardy several items to find in one aisle and bring to the cart. He always had known that his mother was organized, but these last several days brought that realization even more vividly to his mind. Ever the planner, Alice had put an ice chest in the trunk of the car that morning, for holding the milk, cheese, and other food that needed refrigerating. "We'll get your gym stuff and the rest of your supplies tomorrow," she advised him while waiting to check out. "The telephone company said the man would make it to the cabin at one o'clock, so we'd best get back."

On the way out of town, Hardy began looking for kids about his age whom he might expect to meet when school started. It was not easy to tell his age group these days since many of the girls at Jimmy Stearns last year had gotten taller than the boys in his class. Hoping to appear disinterested as he gazed out the car window, the new Pine Gap middle-schooler tried to size up those he saw. No one seemed to notice, although one boy on a beat-up bicycle yelled, "Y'all got a bucket o' bolts!" when they drove by. Hardy rode back to his new home wondering who would be his new friends.

"I saw you in town."

Hardy had just opened his school locker and was trying to place his thick math and social-studies books on the top shelf without dropping his class notebooks on the hallway floor, when he heard a voice that was closer than the others floating past him.

"Yeah, you was sittin' in the front seat of your mama's car, pretendin' not to notice nobody."

He had not had time to turn around to face the person who had just spoken before her husky voice pronounced this frighteningly clairvoyant observation. In the space of a couple instants, Hardy—whose face turned pink faster than it takes a hummingbird to sip nectar—began to whirl around toward her, as his mind was forming the question, "How could she have known?" Before his brain had time to warn him of being off-balance, the new Pine Gap middle-schooler saw his first-day's greatest fear take place.

Like a slow-motion replay, Hardy watched in horror as his class notebooks slid out of his hand. Leading the way toward a sudden and inevitable collision with the floor were the brand-new, sharpened pencils and ballpoint pens that he had placed so carefully inside the notebook pockets. Lunging toward these writing instruments that were hanging momentarily in mid-air, Hardy managed, instead, to slam the notebooks to the floor with a wayward elbow, propel the pens and pencils across the hall to the opposite wall, and lay a most-effective body block across the midsection of his unsuspecting—and as yet unknown—conversation partner. When everything—and everyone—stopped moving, Hardy opened his eyes from an involuntary wincing reflex to find himself staring at a pair of shoes, the feet and legs of which belonged to a female, in whose lap the mortified boy was partially resting.

"This how you introduce yourself?" Hardy realized that the voice was now above his head. Around the two sprawled figures, the moments of silence that followed a few gasps from other students now turned into a burst of nervous laughter.

"Take it out back!"

"Don't take you long, newbie!"

Hardy needed no further prompting. His face practically throbbing red, he tried rolling himself off of her legs as quickly as he could.

"Ow! Take it easy! You want me to dump you on the floor?" The girl's husky voice had turned a bit feisty.

Before Hardy could think of what to say, he felt hands lifting him to his feet. Two girls helped his hapless victim to stand up, but then she shooed them off. "I can take care of muh-self!" The quickly assembled crowd disappeared just as quickly, while Hardy frantically began gathering his wayward school supplies from across the floor. Then he remembered her.

"I . . . I am so sorry about this! I hope you are okay." Hardy looked up at her, absently rubbing one of his elbows as she did the same with one of her knees. She was a little taller than he, wearing what he guessed must have been her first-day-of-school clothes.

Still catching her breath, while checking for wrinkles and marks on her clothing, she replied nonchalantly, "Like I said, you sure knows how to make an entrance!"

Blood that was just beginning to leave Hardy's face raced back. "This is so embarrassing!"

She still had not made eye contact with him, although Hardy had looked her square in the face. "Weren't nuthin'. Anyhow, welcome to *my* world!" She turned and started walking down a hall that now was very empty. "See you 'round school." Then she quickly paused in her steps. "So, what's your name?"

"I'm Hardy."

"Hardly?"

"Hardy!"

"Well, Hardly, I'm Lily Mae. You'd best get to class."

Just then, the bell rang and Hardy couldn't remember which way to go next.

Lingering feelings of his misadventure at the locker seemed to evaporate like morning fog once Hardy and Rusty headed down an overgrown trail behind the cabin. Alice always insisted that her son change out of his school clothes before going outside, so the boy had rummaged through his old jeans and shirts to select an outfit that he would wear for exploring. Boots, cap ("because of the ticks," Alice would remind him), daypack, water bottle, compass, a few snacks, flashlight, and a walking stick completed his necessities. Homework had to be finished first, and he had to wear a watch since Alice knew that it was easy for Hardy to lose track of time.

At first, the greatest fun came in the recollections. He could not remember the first time that he had ventured out in these woods. It must have been with Uncle Rufus, when he was very little. As he and Rusty made their way down the first section of trail, Hardy could tell that it was a place that he and Uncle Rufus had walked many times. He still could see the tall, thin man with the pale-blue work shirt, khaki slacks, and crinkled cowboy hat gliding down the trail as light as a feather. The old leather boots that he wore had made almost no sound on the twigs and dry leaves. His hands were large and thick, gently holding Hardy's hand—sometimes with only one of those huge fingers. Even now, Hardy could hear the old man's voice, strong but soothing, describing a plant, a tree, a bird call, an animal marking, as man and boy discovered the forest together.

Hardy could not have known that his first forays since moving to the mountains would fill him with such fond memories. Being there seemed familiar, inviting, exciting, challenging, and a little spooky, all at the same time! Alice said that she would have to dig around Rufus's papers to find the survey and determine exactly where the property lines were located. Still, they knew from years of visits that the cabin sat in a fairly quiet place. Neighbors were few and far between. Except for the boy's occasional befuddled concentration, Alice did not worry much about Hardy's adventures.

Late-summer weather lingered, keeping the air warm and sticky into the early evening. It was all the excuse that Hardy needed to see how much he could discover in one afternoon. Alice forbade him to pick wildflowers unless there were a bunch of them in one place, and then only one. Rufus had taught him to watch for scat and to make enough noise as he walked and poked around so that any bears in the vicinity would keep their distance.

Rufus had been more than a self-taught naturalist, however. He also had shared stories that he had heard as a child, about people who used to live on this land, with Hardy. For Hardy, these stories were more interesting than a social-studies class. They were about real people who had walked these hills and mountains, built homes, hunted, farmed, and loved their land. Now that Uncle Rufus was gone, Hardy's interest in the forest was turning to these stories. What more could he find out about those days gone by? What else had Uncle Rufus not told him—or not known?

Along one of the tiny creeks, in a fairly flat, small meadow, Rufus had helped Hardy discover his first arrow points. They were not as symmetrical as those on display at the college museum, but he was excited to find them nonetheless. Rufus also had taken him to an old stone chimney, the largest remnant of a house that had burned down years earlier. Large, flat stones from the foundation still formed a rectangular shape, with the chimney at one end. Broken parts of small, clear glass bottles appeared here and there not far from the chimney site. A broken iron skillet stuck out through the hardened ash pile in the firebox. Hardy would try to imagine what the house looked like, what smells came off the cook fire, what the children who grew up there wore and how they played.

Before their first week of cabin life had elapsed, Hardy dug through boxes in his room until he found the old tin can that Uncle Rufus had given him for guarding his forest treasures. On the top of his dresser, he carefully unpacked the can and created a display of some of his favorite pieces: the two largest arrow points, the sole and heel of a child's old leather shoe, the broken neck of a purple glass bottle, a broken china saucer. There was more out there to be found, he was sure of that.

"ALL RIGHT, CLASS, YOU will sit in alphabetical order, by last name. Please start up here with the As—Anderson, Babbitt, Carson, . . ."

Hardy was still keeping his gaze on his feet so as not to attract attention. A few whispers and twitters crept around the room as Mrs. Grimes continued reading the last names of all the students in Hardy's final class of the school day. When he heard "Miller, Newkirk, Nolan, . . ." he shuffled to the next open desk, gliding into its chair and placing his notebook on the writing surface as slowly as possible. Mrs. Grimes was reading "Templeton, Vasquez, Weinstein, . . ." when Hardy felt a poke in his back and heard a whispering voice that sounded vaguely familiar.

"Hey, Hardly, ya doin' awright?"

His eyes and mouth began to spread out over the rest of his face but, fearing any further attention, Hardy called them quickly back to the most military expression that he could muster. He felt a second poke, and the husky voice whispered again, this time more earnestly.

"Hey, you ignorin' me?"

Mrs. Grimes was beginning to talk about the class textbook. Hardy's desire to remain anonymous overtook his usual calm manner. He turned, ever so slightly, glaring at Lily Mae only long enough to spit out under his breath, "I'm fine! Sshhh!"

Seeing that the students in front of him had their textbooks open to the table of contents, Hardy rapidly flipped through the first few pages. Lily Mae calmly opened to the correct page and sat quietly, with a Mona Lisa smile on her face. Hardy exhaled long and hard, checking the desk to his right to see if Mrs. Grimes had moved to a different page.

At the bell, his new classmates poured out of the room, talking and smiling, heading for practices, rehearsals, or buses. "Welcome to Pine Gap, Mr. Newkirk," Mrs. Grimes smiled as Hardy walked by her desk.

"Thank you, ma'am."

"Let me know if you have any questions."

"Yes, ma'am, I sure will."

"See you tomorrow, then," and the teacher returned to the paperwork on her desk.

Out in the hall, Hardy took a moment to figure out which way to walk to his locker. Around the corner, Lily Mae and two other girls stood against the wall, talking and giggling. Lily Mae gestured toward Hardy when she saw him. He looked around and, seeing no one else close by, took a step in their direction. "Come over here! Bein' the first day of school, ya gotta meet more folks."

One of the other girls giggled again. "He the one?"

"Sure 'nuff, girl, but he just shy and nervous. He new here. Name's Hardly."

"It's Hardy," the embarrassed boy sputtered. His hallway audience didn't seem to care, though.

"Glad to meet you, Hardly." "Me, too," the third girl echoed.

"My pleasure," Hardy stuttered, not knowing whether to offer his hand or not.

Lily Mae finished the introductions. "This here's Tawanna and this is Demetria—my best friends. Knowed 'em all my life, here in Pine Gap."

Her two girlfriends were smaller than Lily Mae and, during their introduction, wore oversized grins on their faces. Hardy tried to gain his composure. "Really, I am pleased to meet you. I kinda made a fool of myself this morning in the hall." He turned again to Lily Mae. "I am really sorry for what happened. I hope that you're not hurt."

"Don't worry 'bout me. I'm fine, but be ready for some teasin', 'til the other kids get to know ya." As if on cue, a tall boy walked by, studied the quartet standing by the wall, and grinned at Lily Mae.

"Hey, baby, your new boyfriend? You move fast!"

"Behind the gym, big boy! Behind the gym, any time!"

Lily Mae noticed Hardy's look of surprise at the exchange. "Don't mind him. He just talk."

Hardy smiled weakly. "Well, I need to find my bus. Nice to meet all of you. See you tomorrow."

"See you tomorrow. 'Bye, Hardly." Lily Mae's friends both raised a hand in a small waving gesture as the boy took a few steps backward before turning around. He wandered down the hall, looking lost, until he found the hall to his locker. When he disappeared from view, the two younger girls were still grinning. "He cute," one of them giggled for the umpteenth time.

"Don't be gettin' no funny ideas, hear me?" Lily Mae shot a quick, stern look at her companions. "Besides, you know what folks would say." The three friends then sauntered down the hall to their lockers.

Chapter 4

Maddy

IN THE FIRST FEW weeks after their move, Alice hardly could keep Hardy out of the forest. Checking his homework daily, she knew that he was doing fine with his new classes and studies, so it was hard to come up with a good reason to limit his outdoor time. Besides, she reasoned, autumn meant cooler and shorter days. She wanted Hardy to have as much time as possible to enjoy his newfound passion.

Certainly, she shared in the pleasure of his adventures—mostly stories from the day's experiences with an occasional "find," some new object that captivated Hardy's seemingly unquenchable interest. Colorful stones, fallen bird nests, animal bones, a pecked-out eggshell, and other artifacts were received as new treasures. Hardy was especially excited once when he brought back the left side of a deer rack with four points. His mother helped him mount it over his bedroom door. He needed little encouragement from Alice to begin an explorer's log, complete with dates and detailed descriptions of the day's observations and discoveries. Alice also decided to pick up a brightly colored hunter's vest at the store for Hardy. Deer season was getting close, and she did not want him to end up in the rifle sights of an overly eager hunter.

It didn't take many days out on the trails for Hardy to recall most of what Rufus had taught him. The old man's land was no walk in the park! Its variations and challenges could deceive the eye. Every time Hardy approached the bottom or top of a hill, another change in elevation greeted him. Streams, and even a few creeks that remained steady in summer, crisscrossed the property with an almost indecipherable pattern. Here and there, clearings would appear, flatter parcels than most, inviting speculation as to their history. Since the old stone chimney was in one such clearing, Hardy wondered if early settlers had cleared the other spaces that were still fairly level and uncluttered. If so, how long ago? And where would their water supply have been located? What happened to the houses and barns that must have been around? The few artifacts that he had found near the old chimney whetted his curiosity for more, and not merely for objects themselves. Now Hardy began to think about the people, their lives, and their stories. What happened to them? Does anybody still remember—or care?

One night during dinner, as mother and son were talking about their days, Hardy stopped in mid-sentence and stared at the kitchen wall. Before his puzzled mother could get a word out of her mouth, the boy grinned with his new idea. "Mom, I'm gonna make a map of the forest! I'll bet it's never been done!"

Alice paused with a bite of food in her mouth, absently glancing away for a moment. "Well, probably not in this century," she mused between chews. "I would guess that the early settlers had to have made basic maps, in order to lay claim on sections of land." She paused again. "We might try looking in the county library, to see if it holds any early records and maps. Then you could compare what you work up with the old stuff. That would be quite a project!"

With an energy and excitement that Alice could not remember having seen in Hardy, not even after his soccer team won the Draper championship, Hardy began talking about the trails, the clearings, the outcroppings, and other features that he had discovered since their move. His eyes were practically bulging out of his head, as yet another idea popped up. "And, if I find evidence of a house or barn or something, I could do an archaeological dig! Maybe it would turn out to be such a big deal that it would get written up in *National Geographic*! Wouldn't that be just the greatest thing ever?"

Alice could see that her imaginative son was beginning to hyperventilate, and she worried that he might not be able to sleep that night. "Whoa, there, pardner. You're ridin' mighty fast right now! We'd better make sure that you don't trespass on land that someone wants left alone. Surely Rufus left that survey in his cabin papers. I know the family owns a number of acres here, but let's be sure."

Hardy could hardly hear his mother, his dreams of exploration having expanded quickly in such a short space of time. It was a good thing that he had finished his homework already, for Alice could tell that his mind was gone for the night. He helped her clean the kitchen and the dishes, chatting about one idea after another, as the horizon of his ongoing outdoor adventures kept spreading out. Well, she smiled to herself, the mountains had claimed their latest victim—a man-boy inspired to try to outdo even Lewis and Clark. Still, in spite of her mild frustration, she felt grateful that her son not only had a project of his own, he also was captivated by the spirit of the place. She knew that she was under its spell as well. No wonder, then, as she turned off the lamp next to her bed that night, that she went to sleep thinking about what he might find.

HARDY WAS ABOUT TO discover that the mountains can hold their secrets for a long time.

For the first time since school started, the eager young explorer noticed that the air was getting cool. He had ridden home that afternoon with Alice, dispatched his homework, changed clothes, grabbed his gear, stuffed a few oatmeal-raisin cookies in his shirt pocket (without Alice's knowledge), and galloped out the door. Only Rusty was moving any faster. It was October, and Hardy estimated that he had about two hours of decent light left in the day. Checking the beam strength on his flashlight, he and his canine companion headed down the main trail behind the cabin.

Already, in his mind, Hardy had the outline of his map drawn. He began with the premise that the property was roughly rectangular-shaped. Using his compass for direction, he had selected Cabin Creek as the interim eastern boundary, also fixing western and northern terminal points. As far opposite the cabin as he had explored, Hardy had found a faded, hand-scrawled "No Trespassing or Hunting" sign hanging cattywampus above the remains of a fence that would not have kept out anything on four legs that wanted to be there. As far opposite the Creek stood the old stone chimney. With these points as markers, Hardy estimated that the property was slightly wider than it was deep. Yet he knew it was all guesswork so far.

He also knew that, because of the terrain, it took him more than an hour to traverse the perimeter of the area that he was preparing to map out. He realized that these dimensions meant tens of acres but, beyond that, Hardy's knowledge of measuring property was too limited. This did not bother him, though, since he figured that the overall size would become more obvious once he paced off distances between objects to include in the mapping.

For the better part of an hour, Hardy and Rusty strolled through the middle of the land in question, Hardy recording items of interest in a spiral notebook, Rusty picking up weak scents that led nowhere and occasionally barking at a squirrel or bird. Beams of sunlight were just beginning to throw long, skinny shadows off the right side of the two explorers. Hardy was making an entry in the notebook when he paused, looking up again to get his bearings in what were now, for him, familiar scenes. It was in that moment that he became aware of something new, something that previously he had not noticed.

Instinctively, Hardy sniffed and realized that he was smelling smoke. In those first few seconds of recognition, the boy felt panic crawling up his back, at the prospect of being caught in the middle of a forest fire. He stood as still as he could, while scanning carefully from one direction to another, checking anxiously for any signs of flames or billows of smoke. He saw nothing, so he started sniffing again, calling Rusty to his side. There it was— a distinct and distinctive odor—burning wood. "Wait a minute," he thought, "this smoke does not smell like an outdoor fire. It reminds me of a fireplace."

A fireplace! That could mean only one thing. Suddenly, Hardy became aware that the shadows around them were stretched way out and that he was feeling cold. He glanced down to make sure Rusty was beside him. Fireplace fires are in fireplaces in houses, but how could there be a house out here? Hadn't he walked the whole area by now?

An idea came to him. Squinting into the distance, Hardy looked as high above the tree line as possible, to see if he could detect any signs of smoke. If there was a house with a fire going, a chimney would be creating such a billow. He knew that it could not be behind him, since they had walked that way from the cabin. The curious boy first looked toward the setting sun, reasoning that the smoke would create a silhouette against the bright light. Nothing. Then he looked east, watching for a reverse visual effect. Nothing again. Absently rubbing his forehead with a thumb and forefinger, Hardy shuffled his feet and turned to face in the same direction that they had been walking all afternoon.

What he saw made him jump and catch his breath. It was the "No Trespassing or Hunting" sign that he had seen there on his earlier walks. Yet now it felt ominous, staring down at him from its precarious position on a gangly tree—or was it beckoning to him? Up to that moment, Hardy had not thought about the sign as anything but a boundary marking that he should heed. Now his mind was racing. Was the answer to the puzzle of the smoke beyond this old sign? There was not much time to find out that day. "C'mon, Rusty, let's go see what there is to see. And no barking, you hear?" The trusty pet stayed close to his master as Hardy ducked under a drooping line of fencing wire.

Watching every step he took, to move as quietly as possible through this new territory, Hardy could feel his heart thumping hard. He alternated between soft steps, one in front of the other, and gentle sniffs—nothing that would make a sound. It was difficult for him to tell whether they had been sneaking along for a couple of minutes or an hour, but he knew that light was fading fast. Alice would be looking for him not too long from now. She had not said anything to him about staying out late—not yet. But perhaps he might find the source of this smoke smell in the next minute or so.

Wait! Something caught the corner of his eye. Did a light flicker, up ahead, just now? Was it stationary or moving? Stopping for a few moments to crouch and study the silhouette ahead of him, Hardy could feel his breathing go faster, and his mouth was suddenly very dry. He could tell that Rusty wanted to run ahead, but he signaled the dog to sit. If he looked ahead without moving for several seconds, perhaps he might see that light again.

Yes, there it was! Dim, uneven, but he was sure it was there! Hardy held still as hard as he could and stared without blinking. A window! That light was coming through a window. How far away? The impending darkness was playing tricks with distance and details. Before he knew it, Hardy was hunched over, creeping along the forest floor, heading straight toward the light.

After a few more moments, he could make out the lines of a simple, one-story structure with two large chimneys (one in the middle and one on the far end), a small door at the other end, and the window emanating light in the middle. Hardy started to gasp but caught himself, as Rusty began to growl deep in his throat. A flood of thoughts raced through Hardy's mind as he stood there, about thirty yards away, partially hidden by trees and brush, as silent as a statue.

He had no time to think. Rusty's growl got louder and, before Hardy had a chance to say anything, the big, strong dog began barking loudly. His master knew in an instant that something was up, that something—or some-one—got Rusty's attention. Hardy did not have to wait to find out more.

"Who goes there?" The voice was fierce, growling but not loud, and elderly. Rusty kept barking. Hardy instinctively reacted to hush him, but it did no good. The dog was acting the way that his master felt: scared and threatened.

Then the voice spoke again. "Identify yerself or leave here pickin' lead outta yer hide!"

Over Rusty's almost-frantic barking, Hardy yelled, "My name is Hardy Newkirk. I'm almost thirteen years old, and my mom and I just moved into my Uncle Rufus's cabin way up the hill!"

Hardy's voice seemed to calm Rusty a bit, for his barking slowed. The door to the old cabin opened enough to reveal a squatty figure standing on the middle step, holding a shotgun in one hand, with the muzzle pointed down. Hardy took a quick breath when he realized that the figure was wearing a dress, with a hemline revealing most of a pair of worn, leather boots.

"Newkirk . . . did you say Newkirk?"

"Yes, ma'am, I did." Hardy now could hear just a touch of feminine quality in the crusty, old voice.

"You ol' Rufus's kin?"

"Yes, ma'am, my grandfather and Uncle Rufus were brothers."

Rusty had stopped barking and seemed almost as surprised as Hardy that this conversation was taking place. The old woman standing on the rickety porch paused, pushed the door open with the butt of her shotgun, sighed, and gestured toward the house. "Well, I'd best get a look at cha. Come on in here. It's not much to look at, but I ain't complainin' none."

Hardy looked down at Rusty, who seemed to be waiting for a command from his master. They walked the few steps out of the forest, across what must have been a small yard at one time, and up four uneven wooden steps to the threshold of the door. Just inside, the old woman stood, waiting for them to come in.

An ancient iron cookstove sat near the corner of the room, to the right of the door, its rusty chimney flue making snapping sounds, as the sheet metal warmed from the heat. A door on the opposite end of the room, next to the brick fireplace, must have opened into a bedroom, Hardy thought. A few plank shelves with small boxes and cans, a well-worn wooden counter-top, a basin and bucket, a tall free-standing cupboard, a plain oak table in the middle of the room with a few pine chairs, a rocker that looked like it squeaked with every motion, and a small stack of firewood completed the cabin's interior arrangement.

"Ya don't mind a drink o' well water, do ya, sonny?" The slightly hunched woman was walking over to the cupboard.

"No, ma'am, we have a well at the cabin, too." Hardy had instructed Rusty to sit. The dog obeyed but was still paying careful attention to the old woman.

"Humph! Probably run with 'lectricity. This here's drawn by hand." It was then that Hardy noticed that the room's light was coming from two small lamps, fueled by oil or kerosene. This old cabin had no electricity and, unless it was beyond the only interior door, there was no plumbing in it, either. His hostess poured water from a chipped and faded, blue and white, ceramic pitcher into a tea cup with matching pattern and condition. Hardy wondered if either object had been cleaned lately, but he was polite when she handed the cup to him. "Here, this'll git ya back up that there hill."

"Thank you, ma'am." Hardy cautiously sipped the water and was surprised at how cool and refreshing it tasted. The old woman, whose clothing looked as old as the pitcher and tea cup and whose appearance would have terrified anyone half Hardy's age—especially at this time of year—leaned over and held out a piece of crusty bread to Rusty. He grabbed it quickly and chewed it just as fast. Hardy took another sip of water, as the woman gestured to the chairs at the table. He sat down on one of them as she lowered herself into the rocker, grunting a bit as she settled in.

"Newkirk, eh? How is ol' Rufus? Haven't seen him since last year, believe 'twas." She never really looked at the boy, who thought for a moment that she had been addressing someone else.

Hardy put his head down and cleared his throat. "He died . . . about a year ago. It was cancer . . . kinda sudden." He could feel tears coming, blurring his vision. He blinked them back and hoped that his yet-unnamed hostess didn't notice. She had tipped her head back a little when Hardy had spoken and was sitting quietly, beginning to rub her gnarled hands together. The silence made Hardy nervous. He looked up and was surprised to notice a softness flicker across the old woman's craggy features. He wondered who she was and how she came to be living way out in the woods in a cabin that had seen better days.

"So Rufus is gone now, is he?" She stared off in a corner of the room for a moment or two, that softness almost giving her a warmth that Hardy did not expect. "Pity, it is." Her eyes nearly closed and then slowly opened. "Men like that don't come along much anymore." Hardy felt like he had walked into one of those conversations that adults have in the kitchen when all the kids have gone to bed. Before many questions could jump into his mind, the woman stirred, as though waking from a spell. She looked straight at Hardy for the first time. "So what brings you and your mama up here into these mountains? Ya say yer livin' in Rufus's cabin?"

Hardy felt relieved to have something to say. "Yes, ma'am. We came up here a lot when I was young. Mom loves it up here. She just graduated from college and got her first teaching job in Pine Gap so we could move up here." It didn't seem strange to be telling their story to this stranger, someone with whom he likely would not have addressed if they had seen her in town.

"Ah, yes, I 'member now." Hardy's eyes jumped at this unexpected comment. The gray-haired woman saw his reaction. "I used to see Rufus in the forest, walkin' along like he was meditatin' on things. In the summer, sometimes, he had a little boy with him. Two o' them'd be talkin' 'bout who knows what, and that boy looked really happy. He loved bein' with Rufus; I could see that." She cocked her head, leaned toward him almost imperceptibly, and asked casually, "Don't s'pose ya know who that boy was, do ya?"

Hardy stammered with surprise. "It was me, ma'am." His mind darted back into some precious memories. "I used to walk out here with Uncle

Rufus, as far back as I can remember. He taught me all kinds of things about the woods, the animals, and birds; about the Cherokee who used to live here; about being good to the land." The words had poured out, but now Hardy stopped talking, feeling a little out of breath and light-headed.

In that moment, he thought he could detect a tiny smile tugging on the old woman's face. "Like I sez," she muttered, "he was a good man." Suddenly her gaze moved to the window near the crackling stove. The ancient rocker creaked as her weight shifted forward. Her hands gripped the slightly wobbling rocker arms and began to turn white, as she slowly and with great effort rose up out of the old chair. Hardy jumped up to help balance her, and she did not resist his assistance. When she was standing, she said to no one in particular, "Jus' gettin' old, that's all." Then she looked at him and at the window. "But we'd best be gettin' ya up that hill before ya cain't see yer hand in front o' yer face."

Rusty had jumped up, too, having laid quietly on the floor next to Hardy's chair. Picking up the notebook and pen that he had placed on her table, Hardy shoved them back into the large zippered pouch of his daypack. He pulled out his flashlight as the old woman shuffled to the door. Remembering his manners, he thanked her for the drink of water. "Weren't much, but it'll git ya up the hill." As he walked through the door, Hardy realized that she had not told him her name. He turned and, as if knowing his thoughts, she said, "You tell yer mama that ya just met Maddy Jones. Most folks call me Maddy—they's left that knows me."

Hardy offered his hand, "Very pleased to meet you, Maddy." She extended her right hand, and he shook it gently, without putting any pressure on the arthritic knuckles. He thought he saw the little smile again, dancing swiftly across the woman's face.

"Very pleased to meet ya, Hardy Newkirk. Ya bring yer mama down here sometime, will ya?"

"Yes, ma'am, I'll do that." Boy and dog left the light from the window and followed the flashlight beam toward the main trail. Even though it was the first time that he had walked the woods when it was this dark, Hardy knew where he was. After several minutes of steady progress, he saw a tiny light, up ahead, jumping to a rhythm. He knew it was his mother, so he called to Rusty, "C'mon boy, let's hurry up!" Hardy started jogging the trail, as well as conditions allowed, while Rusty ran ahead, barking.

When the tiny light got bigger, Hardy yelled, "I'm coming, Mama!" Rusty's barking changed, and Hardy knew that the big dog had reached Alice. In another couple of minutes, mother and son met on the trail, both a little out of breath. Alice wasted no time. "Honey, where have you been? I was getting worried when the sun went down."

"Sorry, Mama. I know it's late, but I just met one of Uncle Rufus's neighbors!"

In the dim light, Hardy could see Alice's expression change. "You mean Maddy Jones is still alive?"

"Yes, Mama. Rusty and I ended up at Maddy Jones's house."

Chapter 5

The Graveyard

By the time the two mountain novices had made their way up the darkened trail and back to the cabin, Hardy had filled in Alice on his experience of discovering Maddy's cabin. He could hear concern in his mother's tone of voice, in spite of his animated recalling of the events. She warmed their dinner while Hardy put away his gear and washed up, chatting about one more detail after another. By the time they sat down at the table, said grace, and began their meal, the excited boy had moved beyond the story line to a blow-by-blow description of his feelings from moment to moment.

Alice patiently listened, nodded, and responded here and there, all the while smiling politely. When Hardy finally stopped talking long enough to chew one bite completely before swallowing, Alice put down her fork and gazed at her son. Looking up from his plate, he realized what she was doing. They looked at each other for a few moments, neither of them talking. Hardy was beginning to feel uncomfortable, since he could not remember a time when his mother had looked at him like this. Screwing up his face, he asked, "What is it, Mama?"

She sat still a little longer, not breaking her gaze on him, as though the moment had been frozen in time. Hardy felt a touch of fear, wondering if something was wrong with his mother. Then she eased herself toward the back of the chair and exhaled quietly through her nose. Seeing his curious stare, she realized that she needed to say something. She took another bite, chewed three or four times as if searching for words, and then spoke.

"Son, you are getting older and starting to grow up. I know that I can't protect you from every possible danger in life, so I told myself after your father's funeral that I would raise you to be confident and strong, to be able to take care of yourself. One of the reasons that I am glad that you enjoy exploring around here is that it will help you learn about yourself as you discover things and figure out life." The boy was sitting very still, soaking in every word. He never had heard her speak this way before. Alice stopped talking briefly, and he found himself swallowing with a dry mouth. She smiled at him again and continued.

"Honey, tonight when it was getting dark and you had not returned from the forest, my mind went back to many years ago, to something you can't remember." Another pause, a catch in the throat, and Alice went on. "I remembered the day that the officer came to my friend's house in California, where I was living, and told me that your father had been killed in action." She reached over and took his hand in hers, squeezing it as she spoke again. "I lost one man in my life already. I don't want to lose another."

Gulping like he had just swallowed too big of a bite, Hardy felt his face getting warm and his hands and feet tingling. It seemed like he needed to say something right then. Without a moment's thought, he blurted out, "I'll be careful, Mama, I promise! Don't worry, I promise!" By this time, he had jumped out of his chair and leaned over to put his arms around Alice's neck. He felt a warm tear on her cheek as he embraced her. She sniffed a couple of times as she wrapped her arms across his back and squeezed him gently. "I'll be careful, Mama. Really, I will!"

She cupped the back of his head for a moment in one hand and kissed him on the cheek. "I know you will, son." As Alice let go of her embrace, he did the same and stood up, now looking down at her in her chair. "It's just knowing as a parent that there will be some things that you might not see coming. I can't always protect you." She took his hand again and squeezed it as Hardy looked at his shoes. Smiling once more and dropping his hand, she got up from the table. "Well, now you know what's on my mind and heart, Hardy. Let's warm up your dinner. I imagine it's gotten cold by now."

After dinner and dishes, Hardy tried looking over the notes he had been making for his map, but he couldn't concentrate on them. He pulled out the big tin can and started picking through his artifacts. None of them seemed interesting right then. After absently thumbing through his textbooks, previewing topics for the next day in school, Hardy went downstairs, washed up, and told his mother that he was going to bed. She looked a little surprised but kissed him goodnight, with a smile. In bed, he stared out the window, with his hands behind his head on the pillow, for a long time. Finally, he rolled over and slowly fell asleep, thinking about what Maddy might tell him about the mountains.

In his next several outings, Hardy made a point of arriving back at the cabin just about the time that the sun went down. Fall days meant shorter afternoons for exploring, which meant he was having to plan his trips around available daylight and other activities—like firewood. The wood-shed had a couple of cords of seasoned wood when Hardy and Alice moved in, but Alice did not want to get caught short. Split wood that does not sit out in the sun over the summer gives off less heat in the stove, even hissing and smoking. Heating season was beginning, so the two of them reviewed Rufus's instructions from previous winters from memory and ran a few test fires in the evenings.

To get through the winter and prepare for next, Alice ordered two cords of oak. One was seasoned and the other had been cut recently but not split. Rufus's old maul had been stored in the laundry room, so Hardy agreed to try splitting a cord on his own. On rainy days, he would work under the shed roof, swinging the ten-pound maul head soldered to a hollow metal handle, trying to remember what Rufus had taught him. After a couple of hours of trial and error, Hardy thought that he was getting the hang of the placement and the swing. When some of their Draper church friends came up for a visit, Alice arranged ahead of time for Jack to run electrical conduit out to the woodshed. He then hung a small outdoor light under a corner of the roof, making it possible for Hardy to split and stack wood when it was dark. The boy liked this arrangement since he felt good when he split, and it gave him time to think about his map project.

For all of these reasons, Saturdays were becoming Hardy's major expedition days. He knew that Alice wanted to invite Maddy for dinner but, so far, with the increasing limits on his time, Hardy had not found her at home. The driveway for her cabin headed in a different direction from their cabin, onto a county road that Alice and Hardy had not yet discovered in their drives to town. Hardy had no idea what kind of transportation she had, if any. Until he ran into Maddy again, Hardy was using his outdoor time to fill in the notes and sketches for his map project.

It was on such a day that Hardy stumbled onto a find so unexpected and so astonishing that it changed everything.

Halloween was approaching. Even the middle school in Pine Gap was decorated with an orange and black theme, cutout jack-o-lanterns, small plastic skeletons, and a Halloween cafeteria menu had been published days ahead of time. Some of his classmates were asking Hardy what he was going to wear for the Halloween parade. Alice never had been too keen on the holiday, leaving her son to approach its festivities rather low-key—although he always was happy enough to accept a friend's offer of some trick-or-treat candy.

During the week before Halloween, Hardy split firewood almost every night, polishing his skills at the chopping block and the stove. For this extra work, Alice had agreed that the Saturday prior to Halloween was his for exploring. He was intending to complete his notes and sketches in order to construct the first draft of his map on school nights. Daylight saving time had switched back to standard time, and now weekday jaunts out into the property left little light for detail work. By reviewing his notes and sketches, Hardy decided which locations needed a little more of his attention. Friday night, Alice packed an ample lunch and snacks and laid out a rain slicker for him to include in his daypack. He went to sleep quickly that night, dreaming about someday writing an article for *National Geographic* magazine.

Light was just beginning to give shape to the trees and distant hills as Hardy rolled out of bed and dressed for his day. He walked around in his socks, since Alice had not yet come out of her bedroom, feeding Rusty, pouring himself a bowl of cold cereal with milk and a banana, and poring over his notes and sketches one more time while chewing. His teeth were brushed and his second boot almost laced when Alice stirred, yawning and surprised that her son was about to head out the door this early. She was reciting her list of upcoming Saturday pursuits as he pulled the daypack over his shoulders, adjusted his cap, called Rusty, and picked up his walking stick. "'Bye, Mom, see ya later!"

"Enjoy your day. Be careful!" She pulled her housecoat closer to her neck and walked over to the woodstove. Rusty was not only a good companion for Hardy, she was thinking: he also was valuable protection. Most people or animals would think twice about tangling with a sturdy, ninety-five-pound dog. Holding her hand over the stove, Alice detected faint heat and decided that another few hours of wood heat would be nice. She opened the air supply and, with a few more pieces of wood on the embers, the fire began to blaze again. Then she moved the rocker a little closer to the stove, facing the windows. Pulling a couple of the window shades halfway up, she returned to the rocker and settled in, watching the day begin and warming herself by the fire.

Hardy and Rusty needed the flashlight for the first part of their walk down the main trail. He had learned, the hard way, that wind and rain brought debris on the trails, and the boy didn't want to turn his ankle or step on a branch that would end up in his face. There were three areas of the property that he intended to visit, the first one being a short walk off one side of the main trail. It took him about fifteen minutes to get there and another fifteen minutes to pace off distances, log the rest of the distinguishing features, and indicate in his notes which features of the perimeter corresponded to which other sketches.

Satisfied with his work there, Hardy checked his notes and compass for directions to the second site. It lay somewhere beyond Maddy's "No Trespassing or Hunting" sign and before Cabin Creek. Boy and dog headed off in that direction, Hardy estimating fifteen minutes to destination if they followed a less familiar route and twenty-five minutes if they backtracked and followed the main trail most of the way. Since they had the whole day, Hardy decided to take the shorter way and double-check his drawings of those regions against a different route.

Although he was sure that he had walked every trail and seen the main features of every section of the property, Hardy was surprised by what he was encountering on his route of choice. The terrain was more dramatic than he remembered. Hills were steep, vegetation heavy in one place and then bare, with outcroppings in other places. He kept to his selected route, although it meant difficult, sometimes steeper, climbing at times. Rusty seemed to be enjoying himself, but gradually Hardy began to second-guess his decision and some of his sketches. What was wrong with this part of his previous work?

His face was feeling warm with exertion, and his breathing had picked up, when he and Rusty finally approached the top of what felt like must have been the highest point of the property. Perspiration held the shirt under his coat to his back, as he scrambled the last few feet to a spot that appeared to allow a view of where they had just traveled. Standing on the flattest place at first sight, Hardy drew in a long breath, as he turned around to review their progress. According to his watch, they had been scrambling and climbing for half an hour, longer than his estimate had indicated. And where were they? First he looked out and down, trying to retrace their steps. Satisfied that he knew where they had been, he turned around to see where he thought they should go next.

Trees and brush partially blocked the view, frustrating Hardy and intensifying his curiosity over the sketches, the notes, and their present location. He looked around their immediate vicinity, which appeared to reach a wide, somewhat flat, crest about twenty yards farther from where he was standing. Rusty was trotting in that direction already, sniffing the ground with enthusiasm. Beyond the crest, the terrain appeared to drop gradually and disappear. Then he noticed a couple of features that, taken together, were unlike any other part of the property that he had studied. First, the trees and bushes were smaller than those beyond the crest. This gave the spot a look of having been cleared at one time, and not simply for timber. More morning sunlight slanted its way through the canopy to this spot, giving it an almost eerie appearance. Second, the rocks and stones on the crest itself looked different. Instead of irregular sizes and shapes resting on and poking from the ground, these appeared to have straighter lines and even some curves. They also were closer to being all the same size.

Rusty had returned from scouting the area to check in with his master, who was having trouble making sense out of everything. He pulled the pack off his back and set it down next to one of the stones, lips tight, absently scratching his head through his cap, and beginning to mutter to himself. He decided to check his sketches again, from this new vantage point, to see if he could get closer to finding their bearings.

Stepping back around to pick up his daypack, Hardy stubbed the toe of one of his boots against the stone where it was sitting. The smooth, hefty object tipped over and was knocked most of the way out of the soil, but Hardy was too intent on getting out his hand-drawn maps to notice the floral etchings on one of the stone's corners. He pulled out the graph-paper documents and walked back near the spot where he and Rusty had just ascended. Holding up a couple of the drawings as he surveyed the expanse below, the frustrated adventurer mumbled to himself as he pointed back and forth between drawing and the vista below. He was getting nowhere. Something was missing, as though this new route had made visible a part of the property that Hardy had not seen, let alone paced off. He started to walk back to his pack but stopped again and turned around to face the puzzling terrain in question.

As Hardy stood there, quietly shaking his head and mumbling for a few moments, Rusty had redirected his sniffing to the ground around the stone with the floral etchings. This placed the dog between his master and the daypack on the ground. Suddenly, Hardy turned, expecting to take a step and pick up the pack. Rusty reacted with a muffled yelp and jumped to get out of the way. Hardy lost his balance and, before he knew it, landed face down on the ground.

For a few seconds, Hardy laid still and coughed a couple of times to get breath back into his chest. Then, deciding that he had suffered no injuries (save that of pride), he opened his eyes to get ready to stand up, but he didn't move right away. Above his head, in his line of sight, a stone—larger than the one next to his pack—with flat dimensions had caught his eye. This stone had something carved on it, visible although partially buried in the rough soil. Hardy was beginning to feel the cool ground temperature through his jeans, as he stared at the stone just long enough to realize what he was seeing. Faintly, covered with black moss and weathering stains, appeared a short row of letters!

Before he knew it, Hardy was on his knees, searching for a sturdy stick, then rubbing the end of it over the row of crudely visible letters. When the stick had removed the surface growth and dirt, Hardy dug the pocket knife out of his jeans and began to scrape its shorter blade across the beveled surface. A minute of rapid scraping revealed the distinct shape of the letter "P." Hardy leaned back on his knees for a moment, surveying the stone and thinking. It looked like part of the object was still covered by earth. Grabbing the stick again, he dug around the exposed edges. That stick broke in half, which led to a frantic search for a stronger stick. Perspiration began to appear on his forehead, by the time that Hardy had removed enough of the object to spot another carving.

This one appeared first as a skinny rectangle, with its left side still covered with dirt. More scraping with the stick and, in a few moments, Hardy froze in mid-motion. He was now looking at the carved outline of a cross, about three inches wide and five inches long.

"Jeepers!" he exclaimed. He could feel his heart beating again, just like when he had discovered Maddy's house. He looked at the cross and then back at the letter P. Then he grabbed his pocket knife again and began carefully scraping to the right of the exposed letter. "Sure enough!" he thought after a few moments of scraping. "There it is: a period!" Moving to the opposite side of the P, Hardy scraped there with his knife, too. It took a matter of seconds for another small indentation to appear at that spot as well. "I'm working my way backwards," he noted aloud. "I'll bet I know what is next!" Continuing to the left, he worked with both the stick and the knife, removing more dirt, moss, and the stains of what must have been years of exposure to the weather. Before long, a short vertical line appeared, cut into the stone, just like the letter P to its right.

"One more to go!" Hardy shouted, as Rusty sat nearby, observing with nonchalance the boy's ardent scraping and rubbing on the smooth stone artifact. Hardy uncovered another small, round indentation and was now practically panting, feverishly working his way left. "I see it!" Rusty's ears shot up, and he tipped his head. Within a minute or so, Hardy suddenly stopped, staring at the last section that he had cleaned, momentarily at a loss for words. "I was right! I can't believe it!"

Leaning over for a few more seconds, Hardy quickly reviewed the results of his tedious labors. Uncovered on this puzzling stone object, after who knew how many years, was a carved cross, above which were visible carved letters and periods, "R. I. P." The excited young explorer sounded out the letters, as if learning to read, "R, I, P: Rest in peace!" Then he looked at Rusty, as though his canine companion could appreciate the moment. Throwing his hands up in the air, Hardy yelled so loudly that the dog jumped back a little.

"Holy moly, Rusty! Do you know what this means? There's a cemetery up here!"

Chapter 6

Partners

"Hey, Hardly, where ya goin' after school in such a hurry?"

Hardy recognized the husky sound of Lily Mae's voice, even though at that very moment his mind was ahead of his feet, scurrying, as they were, out of the classroom. He slowed down enough to turn and look at her, just as she fired her second volley. "And what ya writin' in that little book, when y'ain't listenin' to Miz Grimes?"

Lily Mae's powers of observation were beginning to get on Hardy's nerves. She could see that he was hesitating, so she stepped close enough to look him squarely in the eyes, put her hands on her hips, and bobbed her head back and forth, as she scolded and entreated him at the same time. "Look, Hardly, if ya cain't tell me, who ya gonna tell? I'm your best friend here. Sweet Jesus, maybe I'm your *only* friend!"

Hardy realized that it would be of no use to quibble with her. He had had no intention of talking about the forest graveyard with anyone, not even his mother, at least for a while. It was too exciting to think about it! There had been no time since Saturday to return and finish identifying all the headstones that were partially exposed. Hardy was still thinking about his next plan of action once he got a chance to hike back out there. He didn't expect to get lost again, but he couldn't be sure. Anyway, now he was in something of a fix with Lily Mae. She had an almost scary way of picking up on things.

Letting out a deep breath, Hardy reluctantly looked up and down the hall, then grabbed Lily Mae's forearm and walked the two of them toward the wall. By then, Lily Mae was grinning like a spider with a fly at her catch's solemn demeanor. "Well, well, well, this mus' be good, *real* good!"

Hardy looked at her intently, speaking in hushed tones. "You have to promise not to tell anyone . . . not anyone! You promise?"

Lily Mae was still grinning. "I promise."

"No, really! Do you swear on your grandmother's grave?"

"My grandmama still alive. She live with us."

"Okay, your great-grandmother's grave."

"She still alive, too."

The young explorer, who, up to this point, had been content to keep his exploration activities between himself and his mother only, was feeling frustrated. He scowled at Lily Mae and threw up his hands, as much as the books and notebooks in them would allow. "Then what *will* you swear on?"

It was Lily Mae's turn to get serious for a moment. "My pastor say not to swear on nothin'. Your own word be enough. If your big secret be that all-fired important, I won't say nothin' to nobody!"

Hardy studied her face for a moment or two and, when he could see that her patience was beginning to wear thin, he took another long breath. In those split seconds, he went back and forth in his mind, "Should I tell her about the graveyard or not? I haven't even told my mother yet, 'cuz I don't want her to get worried about me out there. If Lily Mae knows, she might get too excited to keep it to herself." Quickly, he decided what he would do. With measured tones, he looked at Lily Mae and declared, "Okay, here it is: I'm making a map."

Lily Mae stared back at him, blinked, raised her eyebrows, and tossed her head to one side. "So?"

Hardy could tell that this quick explanation was not enough for her to appreciate his undertaking. Some elaboration would be necessary. Taking another breath, he continued, "It's gonna be a map of all the property around my uncle's cabin, the cabin where my mom and I live!"

Touching Hardy's forehead with her hand, Lily Mae spoke to him in a soft, cooing voice. "Hey, baby, you feelin' awright? Got a fever or somethin'?"

Rolling his eyes and lifting her hand off of his forehead, Hardy looked her in the eyes again, as if to get her attention one more time. "There's nothing wrong with me! Uncle Rufus showed me an old stone chimney once. That means people used to live out there. I'm going to put in all the streams and creeks and big rocks and trees . . . the chimney . . . and I just might discover something really cool . . . you know, like moonshine bottles, or an old log cabin, or who knows what . . . maybe even an Indian camp!"

His classmate paused, an air of resignation on her face. "Hardly, you got yourself all excited 'bout drawin' some map? Don't worry. I won't be tellin' nobody about it!" She turned and walked down the hall.

It took Hardy a few moments to realize that he could not decide whether to be relieved or insulted. She didn't get it! The map was going to open doors to all sorts of fascinating stories and, eventually, the graveyard could end up the best story of all. Lily Mae was about to turn onto another hallway when Hardy suddenly thought of something. "Hey, Lily Mae!" The tall girl turned around, surprised to be hearing from the boy she left speechless a few moments ago. "Lily Mae! Ask your great-grandmother about liniment bottles!" Lily Mae shrugged and walked out of sight.

For a week or so, the two middle-school students said little to each other. Lily Mae was behaving uncharacteristically quiet around Hardy, but he decided not to badger her. The budding explorer was sure that he could figure out a way to impress her with his extracurricular project. He thought about his can of artifacts, wondering which one might do the trick.

Mrs. Grimes's class was the only one that the two of them shared, during last period. One night, Hardy carefully wrapped something from his tin can and stuck it in his lunch bag. The next day, when the school bell rang at the end of his next-to-last class, he hurried to Mrs. Grimes's room and slid into his seat, watching the door. A minute later, Lily Mae entered. She saw Hardy in his seat in front of hers and kept her gaze on him as she sat down. There was about a minute and a half left before the next bell, Hardy calculated. He swung around in his seat, as inconspicuously as he could, and almost mumbled as he spoke, "I want to show you something I found."

Lily Mae wasn't frowning, yet her expression was serious in a way that Hardy had not yet seen. Leaning forward, she spoke in a low voice. "Listen, I been talkin' to my mama. She a cook at the high school, and she met your mama. Says she a nice lady." Not known for tact, Lily Mae paused to let this revelation sink in. His eyebrows practically touching his hairline, Hardy barely could hide his bewilderment. Lily Mae noted his reaction, exhaled, and continued. "Anyway, she say if I want to go explorin' with ya, we can all talk about it today at the high school."

The bell rang, and Hardy wanted nothing more than to finish this very unexpected conversation. He had not even gotten the "bait" out of his lunch box, an old, curious object that he was sure would convince Lily Mae that his mapping and exploring project was the real thing. It had not occurred to him, however, that she actually might want to be part of it. Sitting up straight, with his face toward the front of the room, Hardy could not concentrate on Mrs. Grimes's voice. He was worried that Lily Mae had broken her promise, that she had let his secret cat part of the way out of its bag.

Minutes dragged by in class. First he began tapping one heel against the floor, then Hardy realized that he was drumming his fingers on the desktop. Gradually, the minute hand moved toward the final bell. When it rang, Hardy immediately whipped his head around and began to speak to Lily Mae intently. "Did you . . . ?"

She interrupted him. "Don't worry. I didn't say nothin' about your precious map, just that you like bein' outdoors and findin' things. She say your mama must be raisin' you right, and it's fine with her if I go with you sometimes."

Once again, Hardy felt that Lily Mae had gained the upper hand. This certainly was not what he had expected to hear. "So . . . ," he stuttered, "so, you want to go exploring with me? Out behind our cabin? You want to find old stuff and help me make the map?"

Pinching her eyebrows together, Lily Mae tried to act disinterested. "Ain't that what I just said?"

His mouth moved silently, as Hardy glanced out the classroom window for a moment. Then his face changed, softening as though the whole scenario was finally sinking in. He turned back to her. "Well, okay! Yeah! Sure! That's a great idea! I'll bet we can find even more things this way."

His new partner in adventure got up from her desk. "Come on. Time to catch the bus, before my mama and your mama get ready to leave." Lily Mae began walking toward the classroom door.

Grabbing his school things and jumping out of his chair, Hardy grinned as he headed out of the room. They were the last two students to leave. "G'night, Mrs. Grimes," he offered in a polite rush.

"Good night, Mr. Newkirk. Good night, Miss Nolan." But the girl was down the hall already. The gray-haired teacher sat watching Hardy's enthusiastic departure, absently holding her chin for a few moments before returning to the work on her desk. She could hear Hardy's rapid footsteps slow down, his voice speaking in a stage whisper, and Lily Mae's boisterous replies. No one was in the room to see Mrs. Grimes smile and shake her head a little.

THE FOLLOWING SATURDAY MORNING, Alice and Hardy drove into town with the directions that Lily Mae's mother had given them for finding their house. Hardy had not been in this neighborhood nor on this street since they had moved to Pine Gap. It reminded him of a couple of areas in Draper, where the houses were small and older, where the lawns often needed mowing and sometimes had a car sitting on them, where kids wore hand-me-downs and played in the street, and where grandparents often sat in lawn chairs on the front stoop or right inside an open garage.

When Hardy saw the street number for Lily Mae's house, Alice steered their car to the curb in front and turned off the engine. Hardy noticed that the lawn was clean, with a few neat bushes and fall flowers. A few small tears and holes decorated the screen door, but the paint on the house looked fresh and the driveway was free of large, dirty oil spots. Hardy looked at his mother and swallowed. "Well, we're here."

Alice smiled. "Yes, we are. You ready to go in?"

Her son fidgeted just a little. "I guess." He looked out the window again at Lily Mae's house. "I've never done something like this before. It's not stupid, is it?"

Alice had one of those knowing looks on her face, as she put her hand on Hardy's shoulder. "Honey, you can be pleased that one of your new friends is looking forward to sharing in your interests. Having friends who are boys and friends who are girls is a good thing." She squeezed his shoulder. "I'm proud of you."

"Okay, let's go. She's probably standing at the window, wondering why we're still in the car." With his head down and cheeks beginning to turn pink, Hardy grabbed the handle and opened the door. Alice's eyebrows raised, but she decided not to say anything else. They left the car and walked up the driveway to the house's front door. As they approached, the door opened, and a smiling woman stepped out. "You must be Hardy! Your mama has told me so much about you!"

"I HAVE MOST OF the property figured out, I think. I've been drawing sections at a time on different pieces of paper. That way, it's easier to get the details onto each one. I started working on one big map, but it's gonna take a while to finish."

"What you find so far?"

"Nothin' real exciting yet—broken parts of glass bottles, iron parts of old tools, . . . and other stuff." He paused, hoping not to have given away to her that he was still keeping a big secret. "And I found Maddy!"

"Who she?"

Alice looked in the rear-view mirror, at the two friends sitting in the back seat, and smiled. Hardy had pulled out all of his drawings, placing them on the seat between himself and Lily Mae, and was shuffling through them almost as fast as he was talking. Lily Mae—taller than the boy, even when sitting—was trying to read whichever handmade map that he had moved to the top of the pile. Her head moved back and forth in rhythm to her host's quick pace. Mention of Maddy shifted her attention.

"Oh, she lives in an old cabin down below ours. It takes about twenty minutes to get there, and you have to watch for the sign she put up by the old fence. Maddy has no electricity, and she heats her house with an old woodstove."

"How old she be, and why she by herself? I never heard of her, and I been in Pine Gap all my life."

"She's really old—got long, white hair and wrinkles on her face. Can't walk too good anymore."

"Maybe the two of you will run into her today, and you can invite her to have dinner with us soon." It was Alice's turn to get in on the conversation.

Lily Mae looked at Hardy for his reaction, but he didn't miss a beat. "She hasn't been around her cabin when I walked by there the last few times, but we could try again today." He turned to Lily Mae, "okay?"

"I'd like to meet this lady. She sound interesting."

"I'll bet she can tell us a lot about the property—maybe even the . . . " Hardy quickly caught himself in mid-sentence, but Lily Mae picked up on his hesitation.

"Maybe even the what?" Her face began to show that look of "you're not gonna hide nothin' from me!" with which Hardy had become all too familiar. He stuttered for a moment and then blurted out what he thought would be a successful diversion.

"The . . . the old chimney! Maybe she knows who used to live there, and what happened to the house, and where we could dig around to look for a big find!"

Lily Mae's eyes squinted slightly, as she read her companion's face. After a short pause, she responded with a tone that she hoped would sound innocent. "Then we go to her cabin today."

"And we'll still have time to look around the stone chimney for old stuff, and walk the perimeter, and . . . "

As the car began the ascent up the cabin driveway, Alice smiled once more.

IT TOOK LITTLE PREPARATION time that morning for the two young explorers. Hardy had arranged all of his drawings and supplies the night before. Alice had found another daypack in a box of their belongings that had not been unpacked yet, for Lily Mae to carry her own sack lunch, a trowel, a few plastic bags, a whistle, and a flashlight. As the two headed down the main trail, with Rusty barking ahead of them, Alice wondered, with some amusement, how much of Hardy's chatter about his explorations Lily Mae was able to absorb. She never had seen him quite this animated about anything else.

Hardy told Rusty to take them to Maddy's cabin, so the big dog took charge of scouting duties while his master regaled Lily Mae with further stories of boy and dog in the big woods. For her part, Lily Mae would listen for a while and then ask questions, probing for more detail on certain points. The boy seemed boundlessly energetic and responded to all of her questions, like a tour guide, sometimes turning around and walking backwards as he talked. Rusty's barking, more than once, directed the two toward the next turn of the trail. Their four-footed escort was standing under Maddy's old sign above the fence, when Hardy finally looked up to realize where they were.

"Time to start watching for Maddy's cabin," he said to his novice hiker. "We might see smoke from the chimney first." He held one of the rusty barbed-wire strands high enough for Lily Mae to duck through it, then Rusty, then himself. Although the sun was out, the air was nippy—cool enough that Hardy figured Maddy would need a fire to stay comfortable. He was right. His pulse increased as he saw a straight, bluish-white billow of smoke in the distance through the trees. "Come on!" he cried behind him. "She should be home this time!" Rusty barked, seeing Hardy's excitement, and ran ahead, while Lily Mae followed Hardy, who was ducking and weaving without a trail, in the direction of the smoke.

When they reached the clearing near the cabin, Hardy suddenly stopped. Lily Mae, following as closely as conditions would comfortably allow, bumped into him and stumbled a bit. "What you doin', Hardly?" Surprise and annoyance tinged her voice.

Hardy's mood had changed. "Sorry, it's just that I don't know if I should holler, to let her know we are here, or just walk on up and knock on the door."

"Don't ya know, it's more polite to knock!" Lily Mae's irritation was hiding a little touch of apprehension. She never had been out in the woods before, but that fact, which she had been able to hide from Hardy, was not going to stop her. Her mouth was feeling dry. She swallowed a couple of times, hoping not to give herself away.

"Then we should walk up there together," Hardy was replying to her, as Rusty barked at the hesitant pair and began trotting toward Maddy's door. Hardy's head turned quickly from Lily Mae to Rusty and, as he saw his canine friend approaching the old cabin, he whispered as loudly as he could, "Rusty. No, boy, no!"

His frantic order was issued too late. Rusty had made it almost to the steps when the door slowly opened. The dog bounded to the top of the small, decrepit porch as Maddy's white head emerged, stiffly raising up and then slowly moving to one side or another. Before Hardy realized it, Lily Mae had grabbed his hand. The door opened the rest of the way and Maddy bent over to greet her visitor. Hardy tugged on Lily Mae's hand. "C'mon, let's go!"

Lily Mae's hand tugged back. "You sure she okay we came here?"

Hardy turned and looked surprised. "Sure she is! I told you she was nice to me when I came before."

"Newkirk? Newkirk? Where are ya, son? Me eyes ain't too good no more."

Suddenly feeling confident, the young explorer looked again at his apprentice and tried to reassure her. "It's okay now. She's lookin' for me. Let's go." He pulled on her hand again but dropped it once the two of them had entered the clearing. As they approached the porch, Maddy was petting Rusty, who had sat down on the porch, enjoying the old woman's attention. When she heard their footsteps, she looked up.

"Aye, ya have a friend with ya today, I can see. Come in, and we'll take care of introductions."

Once inside, Hardy noticed that Lily Mae was gazing about the cabin's interior with a look of suppressed amazement all over her face. Maddy didn't seem to notice as she laboriously moved a couple of chairs for seating. When they all had sat down, Maddy addressed Lily Mae with a tone much softer than he had remembered. "And who might you be, miss?"

"Lily Mae Nolan, ma'am."

"Nolan, it be?" The old woman paused and stared at the warm stove. "Might Ebenezer Nolan have been your grandfather?"

"Yes'm, he was. Died when I was little."

Maddy rocked quietly in her chair for a few moments. "Yes, I knew that. Fine man, he was. Honest . . . gave a good day's labor. Worked for my kin for years. Ebenezer was a credit to his race." She turned quickly to face Lily, "And I mean no disrespect, you understand."

"None taken, ma'am." Lily Mae's reply was smooth and calm, delivered so artfully that Hardy was startled by its polish.

"It's about time your people got a chance, just like the rest of us. Never could stomach lynchin's, and I told my menfolk so." The rocking chair creaked as she shifted her weight. "But they wouldn't listen to me, never did."

Lily Mae sat quietly, almost in a pose. "No ma'am."

Tingling with disbelief, Hardy sat speechless for several moments. He closed his mouth, when he realized that he was breathing through it. Shaking his head a little, he gathered himself and remembered what they had come to do. Rusty put his head on Hardy's thigh, giving the boy a chance to appear composed as he spoke. He cleared his throat. "My mother would like you to come for dinner soon."

"Would she, now?" Hardy thought Maddy might have begun to smile, if only just a little. The bent-over woman leaned forward in the rocker. "You tell yer mama I would be most pleased. Been wantin' to see what ol' Rufus did with that cabin anyway." Then she glanced at Lily Mae and winked. "And will Miss Nolan be there, too?"

Hardy looked over at his companion, who shot back a look of her own that Hardy quickly understood. "Uh . . . well, sure, Lily Mae can come."

In a decisive manner, Maddy spoke once more, as she began to rise slowly from the rocker. "Then you tell yer mama we will be honored to attend. Will Thursday be alright?"

Thinking of no reason to the contrary, Hardy replied, "Sure, this Thursday is fine. I'll tell my mother. She can pick you up while Lily Mae and I finish getting dinner ready." He glanced warily at Lily Mae, who seemed unruffled by the comment.

Maddy appeared oblivious to her guests' silent exchange. "Thank you for the offer. I don't drive no more, and the pickup ain't much to get around in, anyway." She was on her feet before Hardy had thought to assist her and was walking toward the door. Hardy realized that this was their cue, so he stood up as Lily Mae did the same. Before Hardy could say goodbye, Maddy paused with her hand on the door knob and turned toward him. "By the way, when are you gonna show her?"

Hardy blinked at Maddy and then noticed that Lily Mae was giving him one of those "I thought so!" looks. In a last-ditch effort to keep his secret a little longer, he squeaked out, "Show her what?" His sideways glance to Lily Mae was met by one dagger of a glare.

The old woman started to grin, revealing a jagged smile. "Come, come. I ain't lived in these woods all my life for nothin'. You're excited, and with good reason. Let her in on it." Then Maddy's grin dropped. "Be careful, though. They's folks still alive who want the secrets around here kept that way. Understand?" She tipped her head up as she looked straight at Hardy.

"Yes, ma'am. I'll . . . we'll be careful." He decided not to look at Lily Mae again until they were outside and headed back through the woods. "Thank you, and my mother will be by on Thursday night."

"Tell her it's the fourth driveway past yours. About three miles around the mountain, I believe." She had the door open, and all three of her guests picked their way down the fragile steps. Neither adventurer said a word until they had walked beyond the clearing and Rusty was back ahead of them. Sunlight danced through branches to promise a clear day for exploring. Lily Mae held her peace as long as she could.

"What ain't you told me yet? I knew you was holdin' somethin' back on me!"

"Well, what was all that stuff about your grandfather and lynchings? Did you know Maddy already?"

"Ain't never heard of her. But listen, Hardly," she exhaled as she stopped and turned. "Pine Gap a small town. Most o' the folks been here a long time. People know each other's business." The tall girl took another breath and stared at the puzzled boy, without looking into his eyes. "They's a lotta things you don't know or won't understand, prob'ly never *will*. Readin' 'bout 'em ain't the same, and that's not countin' the things that nobody puts in them books."

Hardy got quiet for a few moments. "But you can talk to me. I'll listen, I really will."

"Maybe you will, maybe you won't." Lily Mae's eyes looked fierce but very moist. Her lips pulled tightly against her face, scarcely quivering, her arms folded tightly across her chest as she looked away from Hardy. He thought she might cry, but she looked too determined to let herself go there. He stood motionless, too, saying nothing. Rusty, noticing that they had stopped walking, trotted back and sat at attention. Lily Mae stood silently for a few moments longer, exhaling deep breaths, while Hardy began to wonder what to do next. Suddenly, with her arms still folded, she looked over at Hardy with a characteristic expression. "What you not told me yet about this place? I knowed you was hiding somethin'!"

Words stuck in Hardy's throat for a second or two. "Uh . . . okay . . . but you have to promise not to tell anyone, not your mama, not my mama . . . not anyone! Not until I say it's okay!"

Lily Mae rolled her eyes. "We been through this already. Just tell me, okay?"

Hardy shifted his daypack and started walking. "I won't tell you; I'll show you. Let's go, it's gonna take a little while to get there. This is not what I had in mind today."

Lily Mae quickly caught up to him and jumped in. "If we gonna be partners, I gotta know everything."

"Okay, okay. But this hike is a little tough in places. Are you ready?"

"Hardly, anywhere you go, I can go!"

"Then follow me! C'mon, Rusty, let's show her the biggest surprise so far!"

"And one more thing: don't think I be grabbing your hand every time I get scared!"

Hardy blushed, but she couldn't see his face right then. "'Course not."

Chapter 7

Names

He knew that it would take the two of them at least a half hour to get from Maddy's cabin to the secret graveyard—probably more, Hardy thought, since he didn't know how Lily Mae would do. Some of the distance could be traveled by trails that Hardy already knew, but the young adventurer remembered all too well the scramble that he and Rusty faced just before they found the cemetery site. Too, he was a bit worried that he might lose his bearings on the way. This was his first chance to return there since that very unexpected discovery. Thoughts, pictures, and feelings crowded his mind— of not getting lost, of not losing Lily Mae, of trying to remember locations of the headstones that he and Rusty had uncovered, of wondering if and how they would be able to find out about the people buried there, once they made a list of names.

"Hey, Hardly, wait up!" Lily Mae's voice interrupted Hardy's somewhat absent-minded traipsing. He turned to look back and saw his companion some distance behind him on the trail, puffing and taking exaggerated steps, in danger of losing her balance. Hardy ran back, looking for something on the ground that would work for a walking stick. Seeing him coming in her direction, Lily Mae stopped, trying to catch her breath and wiping her forehead with her jacket sleeve. This was not a moment for admitting defeat, however, so she went on the offensive. "You goin' too fast. I ain't been on this trail before!"

"Sorry," Hardy replied, as he handed her a slightly bent oak limb that he just picked up. "Here, I forgot to get you a walking stick. This should work for now. If it's okay, we'll clean it up later and keep it at the cabin." Lily Mae took the limb and tested it on the ground in front of her, maintaining a mild scowl on her face for good measure. Rusty barked at the two when he heard them talking far behind him. Hardy's mind had slowed down by then, and he apologized once more. "I guess I was thinking so much about getting to the cemetery that I forgot about this being your first time out here."

"This'll do." Lily Mae finished tapping one tip of the limb several times against the trail in front of her and then leaned on the other end, to test its strength. "Okay," she exhaled, "how much farther?" Hardy noticed that her tennis shoes had gotten pretty dirty and that perspiration still glistened on her forehead.

"Well," the amateur mapmaker hesitated, "I don't know for sure. I've only been up there once." He paused, turned his gaze away from Lily Mae and looked down at the ground.

Lily Mae's eyes began to light up. "You don't know where we goin'?"

"It's not that," Hardy stuttered, his pride slightly wounded. "I kind of found the place by accident, but I still don't have a clear route figured out for it, even though I stayed up there a while and walked home in daylight."

Thumping her makeshift walking stick on the ground once more, Lily Mae tried to regain the upper hand. "Hardly, I ain't walkin' 'round in circles if you don't know where to find this so-called surprise."

Hardy played the only card that he thought would work. "Don't worry. It will be worth it, I promise!" He gestured with his hands for extra effect.

Wiggling the top of her new wooden trail helper as though checking its strength again, Lily Mae appeared unconvinced. "Better be. Maddy said so." She shot him a quick, sideways glance.

"Maddy's right!" Hardy thought their conversation had turned his way. He pulled off his daypack and dug through it, talking as he looked. "Just to be sure we don't get lost, I'm gonna look at the maps again." Lily Mae snorted as Hardy checked their bearings, mumbling to himself about adjustments for this and that, turning first one piece of wrinkled graph paper and then another back and forth. "Okay," he offered as a final note of persuasion, "now I've got it. We should be fine. Let's go!"

"Don't walk as fast," his novice hiker protested as Rusty jumped up to run ahead again. The three of them continued on one of the main east-west trails for about twenty minutes, Hardy checking on Lily Mae more often, Lily Mae taking advantage of the wooden third leg that Hardy had found for her. Her wind had improved by the time that they turned off the trail, and Hardy used his compass to choose their way through unmarked territory. Lily Mae stopped once to take a drink of water from her canteen. Hardy thought that was a good idea and did the same. When they approached the spot where Hardy had had to scramble uphill, he let Rusty pick the way, and the two of them followed the dog. Rusty seemed to know his assignment, as he made an invisible "S" pattern up the slope, rather than charging in a straight line. Hardy was surprised at how much easier the ascent seemed to go this time.

It took only a few minutes for the three of them to reach flatter ground. Lily Mae had been relatively quiet since receiving her walking stick. When she saw that Rusty and Hardy were now standing still and looking back at her, she grunted, "We there?"

"Just about!" Hardy waited for her to reach them and then turned around as he gestured to Lily Mae. "Now, as we walk slowly in this direction, tell me what you see." He had a big grin on his face as he took his first steps, watching Lily Mae next to him.

"What big secret I gonna see, Mr. Adventure Man?" Lily Mae's jibe went unnoticed, as Hardy alternated between watching his own progress and waiting for a visual reaction from Lily Mae.

"Well, do you see anything yet?" The excitement in his voice was unmistakable, but Lily Mae kept walking, deadpan. Hardy stayed quiet, leading them in one deliberate step at a time. Suddenly, Lily Mae jerked back in her tracks and grabbed Hardy's forearm. Her eyes grew big, and the oak-limb-turned-walking stick tottered to the ground. Hardy turned quickly to watch her.

"Sweet Jesus, Hardly! They's dead folks buried up here!" He could feel the squeeze of her hand tightening on his arm.

"It's a cemetery, Lily Mae! A really old one! I don't think anybody knows about it anymore. The headstones are mostly covered up with dirt. I found the first one when I tripped over Rusty, so I looked for as many as I could find and started digging them up."

Lily Mae looked at Hardy with such fright that he thought at first she was playing with him. "You dug up ol' graves? You crazy or somethin'?"

"No, no—not the graves, just the stones. Don't ya see? If we find different people's names, and especially when they were born and when they died, we might be able to find out about them! Maybe there's an old book at the county library that tells about 'em. Maybe some of my ancestors are buried here; I think we're still on Uncle Rufus's land." For the first time, Hardy was talking about his big secret and didn't have to hold in all of his thoughts and ideas about the cemetery discovery.

However, Lily Mae was not ready to listen to it all. Her hand dropped from its clutch of his arm, and her voice assumed a much more familiar tone. "Now hold on, Hardly. You sayin' you want me to help you clean dirt off these ol' gravestones, sittin' here on top of all these ol' rottin' bodies, just to find their names and then look 'em up in some ol' book?" She paused, as if to hear what she herself had just said. Then she made one of those faces that babies make when they take a bite of something that doesn't taste good. "How creepy is that?" She took a couple of steps back, still tasting the unpleasant thought.

Hardy frowned. It was obvious he was not convincing Lily Mae that the cemetery was an exciting find. What could he say or do to change her mind? Then he remembered the conversation in Maddy's cabin only an hour earlier, when Maddy unexpectedly hinted at the subject of the secret cemetery. Why would she have done so? Surely not to spoil Hardy's fun! Suddenly, in one flash of an instant, he had an idea. Imagining himself with the confidence of Matlock, Hardy looked at his reluctant associate and pursed his lips, "Lily Mae, you said that your family has lived in Pine Gap for a long time, right?"

The tall, tired girl blinked at her questioner blankly. "What you up to, Hardly?"

"Well, maybe Maddy knows something about your family history that we could discover in this cemetery. After all, she knew your grandfather." It was a wild idea, he thought, but if it got her back in the game, it would be worth it.

Lily Mae was not ready to be persuaded. "Boy, you don't know nothin'! My people ain't never been buried with th' likes of your kinfolk!" She glared at him with a triumphant, yet still inviting, air.

Sensing a line of argument, Hardy took her challenge. "How do you know for sure? Maybe there is a reason this cemetery is gettin' all grown over, with nobody taking care of it. Maybe a long, long time ago, things were different." Then he decided to hedge his bets a little: ". . . at least for a while."

On the outside, Lily Mae appeared to be as dug into her point as she ever could be, but Hardy thought he detected a slight change in her expression. Pulling off his pack and digging through it as he talked, he moved gingerly to his next point of persuasion. "See, I read once that you can take wax paper and make rubbings of headstones." From his pack, the boy lifted out a roll of wax paper that had been stealthily removed from his mother's kitchen. As Lily Mae stared, speechless, first at the wax paper and then at her animated companion, his hand drew from the pack once more, this time holding a small carton of crayons. Seeing that his schoolmate-turned-novice-explorer's mouth was hanging open, Hardy capitalized on the moment to continue. "Charcoal is supposed to work good with rubbings, but mom doesn't have any charcoal pencils around the house. I figured these crayons would work pretty well."

The art teacher's son looked up just in time to see Lily Mae's face change. When she spoke, Hardy took a step back and suddenly realized that his fortunes had reversed again. "You crazy? Ain't nobody talkin' me into hunchin' over no grave and rubbing a crayon over th' stone!" Her arms were folded by then, and her back was starting to turn away from the boy.

Even though he was losing ground quickly, Hardy came up with yet another idea, one that he thought might save the opportunity. "Okay, okay! You don't have to touch anything you don't want to touch." She was standing still by then. Perhaps, he thought to himself, he might be recovering his advantage a little. "How about if I do all the headstone work, and you can write down what's carved on them when I read it out to you. Are you willing to draw a map that shows where we find every stone?"

Curiosity and adventure began to creep back onto Lily Mae's face. Audibly exhaling, she looked at Hardy's feet as she spoke. "I can do that, but I want to find things, too, ya know—ol' stuff."

Now Hardy felt they were getting somewhere. "Okay . . . uh . . . how about if I show you some spots up here that don't have any headstones on them, and you can do a little digging to see if people left bottles or plates or somethin' up here. Ya know, people used to have picnics in cemeteries."

Lily Mae shivered. "Just give me one o' th' notebooks and somethin' I can dig with." Her eager-beaver trail guide and amateur-archaeologist friend was too absorbed in what seemed like a rare victory to give much thought to Lily Mae's condition at the moment. He did not see the tremble, nor did he notice the cool touch, of her hand as he gave her a notebook, pencil, and trowel. She followed him quietly as Hardy walked beyond the area where exposed stones were visible. "It looks like there is a row of rocks here. They might be a border for the grave area. Anywhere over there," he gestured the other direction, "would be a place to look around." He kept thinking aloud. "Maybe if you did some walkin' around, you might see some things stickin' outta the ground. I haven't looked over there. Oh . . . " he thought of one more thing in his pack that Lily Mae might use and pulled them out. "Here, these might help you uncover spots that look interesting." He handed her a pair of garden pruners, which she took with a mumble.

Hardy walked back into the section with the visible headstones and left Lily Mae standing alone. Her pulse rate was returning to normal. She took one more deep breath and exhaled, taking a step or two in the direction to which Hardy had pointed, holding the items that he had clumsily placed in her hands. Glancing absently right and left, she bent down on one knee, laid the notebook, trowel, and pruners on the ground, and wondered where to begin. Hardy's voice distracted her for a moment, as it called from a short distance away. "I think what I'll do is uncover all the headstones I can find and then read off to you whatever is on each one. Then I can go back and rub the ones that look the most interesting."

Lily Mae barely sounded attentive and grunted an almost inaudible reply. A few moments later, she swiveled around on her knee and barked, "Hey, Hardly, how much we tryin' to do here today?"

His head popped back into sight. "I dunno. Probably won't have time to finish the rubbings, so we'll have to come back." His eyes darted back and forth for a second or two as another thought came to mind. "I sure hope you find somethin' over there."

Clipping away some tall, dry weeds, Lily Mae asked, "Why?"

"So we have somethin' to show our mamas. That way, they won't start askin' questions. We could tell them we spent most of the day walking all over the place. But I'm not ready to tell 'em about this yet."

Lily Mae was starting to feel more like herself again. "What you gonna do first? Make a big report in social studies? 'Hey, class, on weekends I dig around in graveyards!'" She looked up to see how Hardy would react.

Busy massaging another dirty headstone with a strong stick, Hardy seemed to miss her intent. "I'd really like to find something special first! Just think what might happen if word gets out. Other people might want to see this place, even though it's on private property." He paused again, aware of the deluge of images and thoughts that had been rushing through his mind since Maddy had verbally nudged him earlier that day. "Anyway, maybe all the old-timers around here already know about this place and don't care about it anymore."

His comments left Lily Mae surprised and quiet. She decided not to say anything else right then, turning back instead to the spot where she had been clipping tall weeds and tapping into the soil with a small stick. A few dull thuds here and there located an occasional hand-sized rock not far under the surface, which the fourteen-year-old would discard impatiently. Occasionally, Hardy would make comments to no one in particular. Lily Mae pretended like she didn't hear him, until one of her quick jabs into the rather soft soil yielded a dull "ping" sound. She pushed her probe stick in the ground again, near the same spot, this time a little slower. The ping now sounded like a "clink." Using the stick to dig, Lily Mae needed only a few more seconds to open up a hole in the dark earth and catch glimpses of an object that clearly was not geological.

Before she knew what she was doing, the now-excited teenager hollered out, "Hardly! I think I got somethin'!" Dropping his stick tool, Hardy jumped up and ran over to where Lily Mae was using the end of her short stick, scraping around the object, to identify its size and shape.

"What is it?" he shouted as he knelt down next to an almost-feverish Lily Mae. By this time, she had the stick pushed underneath the smooth-surfaced object and was trying to pop it out of the ground. Her stick broke, so the two of them frantically searched the immediate vicinity for a stronger replacement. Lily Mae found one and quickly employed it to rub more dirt off of the object's top surface. Something on the surface grabbed the stick momentarily as Lily Mae rubbed it from one end to the other. She switched tactics, working the stick underneath the object, as Hardy exclaimed, "Oh my gosh! It's writing! There's words on it!"

Lily Mae held her breath for a few seconds, as she gently but steadily pushed down on her end of the buried stick. Then, without warning, the object of their intense attention flipped out of its hole, hanging for a moment several inches in the air above its unintended tomb. Before it could return to the ground, Hardy had scooped it up with his hands. "An old bottle!" Lily Mae declared, as Hardy used his thumbs to remove the rest of the soil. Now they could see that their discovery was about nine inches long and about an inch deep, made of thick, clear glass, with a short neck, a flat bottom, and beveled sides. Hardy could feel ridges on the flat side, which they now could see formed raised letters on one side of the bottle. In another moment, the mystery was solved.

"Foster's W. C. Liniment," they read aloud, together, and then Hardy handed the bottle to Lily Mae. Still kneeling, with a detectable smile on her face, Lily Mae slowly turned the bottle over and over in her hands. Hardy was grinning as she turned to him and said, "Boy, you wasn't kiddin'!"

"About what?" He was still grinning.

"About lin'ment bottles! I just found one!" He never had seen Lily Mae look this delighted.

For the next few hours, a pleasant mood settled over the two young explorers. Lily Mae would decide on a spot where she wanted to dig, while Hardy was clearing off several more of the headstones. Occasionally, he would bark out a name, dates, and any sayings from the stone that he had finished cleaning, while Lily Mae wrote the information down on a sheet of paper coded to a crude map that she had drawn. They finished their lunches by the time Lily Mae had also found a couple of ceramic buttons, an old marble, a rusty belt buckle, a small, iron hammer head, and a short, thin, smooth piece of metal shaped like an "S." As each of these items emerged from the ground, Lily Mae would yell out and Hardy would come running. The two would then talk loudly, to no one in particular, as they turned the object over and over in their fingers.

Finally, Hardy stood up after reading off yet another headstone to Lily Mae and looked at his wrist watch. "I guess we'd better head back before the sun gets low." Lily Mae was using her jacket as a pad for her knees, while continuing to dig. Perspiration was evident on her forehead, and when she looked up to reply to Hardy, he could hear her huffing.

"Just wanna find one more o' somethin'." The stick made curious little sounds every time Lily Mae gingerly pushed it into, and then pulled it out of, another place in the ground around her. Occasionally, she would put the stick down and run the palms of her hands across the top of the ground, as though she were smoothing out a bedsheet. Hardy was struck by how quickly she had established a search technique, musing that he had never seen her this intent about anything. He realized that she could use a pair of gloves, to protect her hands. Glancing at his watch again, looking up and around at nothing in particular, he rubbed his forehead with the back of a hand. "Well, I want to clean up everything we find today before we take you home, but I guess we could stay fifteen more minutes."

Lily Mae never looked up, moving her jacket several feet away and starting up again. "Okay." Hardy went back inside the cemetery border, pulled some papers out of his pack, and reviewed sketches. When fifteen minutes had passed, there were no new discoveries and the two would-be archaeologists started packing up. Lily Mae wrapped each of her finds in a piece of newspaper and placed them carefully in her pack. Hardy called for Rusty, who liked to do his own exploring, and the big dog quickly appeared, bounding out of the thicker bushes not far away. After a gulp of water from their canteens, they followed Rusty toward the main trail and back to the cabin.

Alice was excited to see and hear details of Lily Mae's discoveries, although the two junior-high students had decided on the return trail how they were going to tell the story. Nothing was to be said of the cemetery, only that both of them had spent time digging around the old chimney (which Hardy had done already). Their plan seemed to work, as Alice asked no questions that would have required a significant degree of fibbing to protect their secret for the time being. Almost as an afterthought, Hardy remembered that they had spoken with Maddy about Alice's dinner invitation.

Alice smiled when she heard his report. "Thursday night it is, then," she said as they all were walking out the back door toward the car. "Oh . . . and I will be inviting Mr. Hunt to join us."

Hardy looked at Lily Mae, who furrowed her eyebrows and nodded her head in Alice's direction, as the two of them climbed into the back seat of the Maverick. Hardy paused, but Lily Mae repeated her head gesture. "Who's Mr. Hunt?" the boy asked, trying not to sound puzzled or nervous.

Turning on the car's engine, Alice didn't miss a beat. "Oh, you remember, I introduced you to him one day after school, when you came by my room." Hardy and his back-seat companion looked at each other again, he with a puzzled expression and she with a Cheshire-cat smirk. Nudging him in the shoulder, Lily Mae shot her eyes between Hardy and his mother a couple of times. Hardy finally got the hint.

"Oh, that guy. Well, he seems nice."

Alice's knowing grin could not be seen from the back seat. "His wife died a couple of years ago, and I think he would enjoy meeting Maddy."

"Sure. Yeah. Sounds good." Her son was too busy fending off Lily Mae's teasing to pay much attention to what he was saying. When the tall girl made a kissy face, Hardy tried to punch her on the shoulder, but she caught his fist and wrestled it back to his side of the seat. Hardy mouthed out the words, "Stop it," but Lily Mae hardly could stop herself from bursting aloud in laughter.

"Everything alright back there?" Alice's voice sounded innocent, but it was enough to settle Hardy down.

"Sure, Mom, fine." He glared at Lily Mae, who made one more kissy face and grinned widely at him before turning toward the window. Hardy could see the heaves of her shaking shoulders for another minute or so, but he knew he was helpless to do anything about it. For the rest of the ride, he thought about the events of the day and what they had found. He wondered when the right time would come to share news of the cemetery. Surely, he thought, Maddy would keep it quiet for now.

Chapter 8

Dinner with Maddy

"HARDY! WOULD YOU OPEN the front door for Mr. Hunt and Maddy, please?"

Lily Mae and her young host were setting the table, when a knock was heard from the front door. Hardy left Lily Mae to finish the silverware, as he walked the width of the expansive living room and let in their guests. Mr. Hunt had Maddy's arm in his as they greeted Hardy from the porch. Alice was wiping her hands on a kitchen towel as she met them inside the door.

"Welcome, Miz Jones! Mr. Hunt, thank you for offering to pick her up. I am pleased to have all of you," she turned and gestured Lily Mae's way, "here for dinner tonight! Please come in from the cold."

Everyone gathered in the living room for a few moments, as greetings and introductions were made all around. Hardy was impressed with how elegantly Lily Mae conducted herself. She had ridden home after school with Alice and Hardy and was helping Alice in the kitchen, while Hardy brought in more firewood and stoked the stove. Once the meal was under control, Alice showed Lily Mae to her bedroom, so the girl could change into the clothes that she brought for dinner. She put on a dress, sweater, black leather flats, and makeup that didn't look overdone. Meanwhile, Alice had scooted Hardy upstairs to put on "Sunday clothes," which he reluctantly did.

As the five of them stood together for the first few moments, Hardy noticed how different Maddy looked. She was wearing a long dress and shawl, with her hair up in a bun, and a necklace of small stones and beads. Both the dress and necklace looked quite old but still rather striking. Hardy thought he could see more of Maddy's face, which now looked softer as she smiled and appeared pleasantly old-fashioned with her greeting rituals.

Mr. Hunt sported a tweed jacket and slacks, with a light overcoat slung over one arm, looking pretty much the same as he had looked the day Hardy met him at school, but missing the necktie. His face was craggy but warm, wearing a smile that reminded Hardy of the way family members acted at their beloved Uncle Rufus's funeral. As the two of them shook hands, the boy could feel a tingle in his hands and feet.

Alice was completely at ease with the occasion and her guests. "It's a little early in the month," she offered, "but I think we can call this a Thanksgiving meal. I, for one, am thankful to be here and to know each one of you." She smiled again at each guest and put her arm around Hardy's shoulder. "Hardy will take your coats. Please, have a seat at the dinner table." Hardy and Lily Mae had decided earlier in the day who would sit where, so Lily Mae walked Maddy and Mr. Hunt to their chairs, while Hardy dispatched evening wraps.

For several days, Hardy had been looking forward to the meal that now was coming to the table. He and Lily Mae brought dishes from the kitchen—mashed potatoes, gravy, pot roast, fried okra, creamed corn, Caesar salad, bread, butter, and jelly, with sweet and unsweet tea to drink. For dessert, Alice had baked a pie with apples they had picked at a local orchard. After saying grace, Alice started passing dishes and talking with everyone. Until that night, Hardy could not remember having seen his mother in such a charming, almost elegant, role. Once each guest had food on their plate, Alice turned to the one guest whom she had not yet met.

"May I call you 'Maddy?'"

"Please do."

"Maddy, I am very pleased to meet you and to have this occasion to talk with you. Hardy's Uncle Rufus mentioned that he had a neighbor or two in the vicinity, but I never took the time to find out who they are. I gather that you have lived here for many years." Hardy was working on his first big bite of pot roast and mashed potatoes, but he was all ears for Maddy's reply. Lily Mae took a bite of the okra and chewed politely as the elderly woman spoke.

"All my life . . . was born in that cabin. Papa and Mama had seven children. I'm the only one left."

As Maddy paused to take a bite, Hardy jumped in with a question that was on his mind. "Do you keep your cabin warm with that one woodstove? How can you get enough wood?" A jab on his shin from the side of Lily Mae's foot brought Hardy's line of questioning to a halt. Alice glided right in behind his words.

"Hardy is impressed that you are so skilled at heating with wood."

"It's all I know. Learned it as a young'un, just like with haulin' water from the well and lightin' a kerosene lantern. The boys split and hauled the wood. Mama taught the girls how to cook and bake with wood. Got a couple o' nephews who keep me stocked with dry firewood."

Mr. Hunt jumped in. "Yes, the Jones family is legendary around Pine Gap. Maddy's ancestors were some of the first settlers here. I imagine she is a treasure trove of old stories, and I hope she has been passing them on to the next generation." He smiled at Maddy approvingly.

Swallowing a bite of food, the guest of honor faintly grimaced, in a way that reminded Hardy of the first time that the two of them had met. "Ain't interested—not none of 'em." Lily Mae and Hardy looked at each other.

Mr. Hunt continued. "Maddy, the high school social-studies department has a project for preserving the heritage of this area. Would you be willing to tell stories to a couple of my students, so they could record them for posterity?"

The old woman was chewing another bite and appeared not to hear his question. Hardy and Lily Mae exchanged glances once again. Finally, Maddy swallowed and cleared her throat. "Well, I s'pose if a couple o' your students want to listen to an old woman talk about the days gone by, shan't hurt nothin'." Both youngsters looked visibly relieved, as Mr. Hunt responded to Maddy.

"Wonderful! I will make arrangements and get back with you."

"Don't have a phone. Just tell young Newkirk, and he," she paused to look at Lily Mae, "and his lovely friend can bring me the details." Hardy turned to gauge his friend's reaction, but Lily Mae sat quietly, with her Mona Lisa smile. Maddy, however, had more to say. "By the way, Richard," (it was the first time that Hardy had heard the social-studies teacher's first name) "I was sorry to hear of your wife's passing. A fine young woman she was. Her kinfolk and mine go way back."

Hardy thought he saw Mr. Hunt flinch. He took a moment before replying, "Thank you, Maddy." He exhaled. "It was very hard to watch her go like that—hard for the whole family. But it's been two years already, and she kept telling her family and friends to go on living, so we are making the best of it."

Before Hardy could form the words in his mind, he could feel Lily Mae's foot jabbing his shin again. He looked quickly at his mother, whose eyes seemed a bit glassy right then. She was getting ready to say something.

"Mr. Hunt is a wonderful teacher. He makes history interesting for the students. Pine Gap is fortunate to have him."

The widower looked down at his plate and smiled a little. "Those are kind words, Alice. I'm not a local, but Betty's family has been good to me." Hardy took another bite, just to keep his mouth from hanging open.

Alice turned once again to Maddy. "So, Maddy, what is one of the most interesting early stories that you remember about this area?" Hardy stuffed in more potatoes, along with some creamed corn.

Glancing almost imperceptibly at the two young explorers, the old woman finished chewing a bite and put her napkin next to her plate. "Well, now," she smacked her lips as if for effect, "it would have to be Cherokee Ben." She paused, and Hardy was sure that Maddy shot another pair of knowing glances at Lily Mae and himself. The boy could feel his heart working overtime. "Yes, Cherokee Ben lived more than a hundred years ago. Brought his family to the Moravian mission and helped the missionaries survive their first winter. Had a farm of his own, a bunch of kids, even more after his first wife died. Got married a second time after the government run out all the Cherokee, but some hid in the mountains and didn't go to Oklahoma. Ben was one of 'em, kinda like their leader, even though they had to lay low for years." She stopped talking for a few moments, and once again Hardy had the feeling that Maddy was giving the two youngsters some kind of signal.

"What happened to him . . . to Cherokee Ben?" The adventurous boy's curiosity couldn't hold him back, not on such an intriguing story as this one. He looked quickly again at Lily Mae, who had put her fork down, and Alice, who was looking at Maddy, with one hand under the other elbow and the other hand under her chin.

"Nobody knows for sure. At least, that's what they always said. Same with the mission. The Moravians left soon after the Trail of Tears and nobody came back." She sighed quietly. "Shame, too. They was good people. Had been around long enough to bury some of their own."

Hardy was afraid that Alice would hear his heart pounding all the way across the table! As she entered the conversation, the new art teacher appeared not to notice. "You know, that reminds me, when we were moving in here before school started, we found a small leather journal, in Uncle Rufus's handwriting. I flipped through a few of the pages, and it looks like he used it for writing down things he remembered about this property and its history. Perhaps," she turned to Hardy, "that book has some stories that go as far back as the mission and Ben."

Hardy thought he was going to explode. Shoving food into his mouth was not helping, so he started tapping his foot under the table. Alice noticed that he was getting a bit wiggly and gave him a quick, discreet look that parents know how to deliver in social situations. Slowing his chew, Hardy turned his head in Lily Mae's direction, expecting to find her still perfectly composed. Mostly she was—a calm expression, chewing quietly, sitting up straight in her chair. He was surprised, though, to see Lily Mae's hands in her lap, twisting her cloth napkin, first one direction and then another. She, too, was excited about something.

"Hardy?" The boy suddenly realized that his mother had been speaking to him. "Hardy, do you remember where we put that book?"

Realizing that he had food in his mouth, Hardy swallowed before trying to reply. "Uh, I think so." His mind was rushing helter-skelter. He couldn't recall for sure where the book was, but he figured that a "maybe" was a better answer right now than a "no" and more honest than a "yes." His stomach was jumping so much that even the thought of apple pie did not sound good.

"Well, we certainly will want to read through Rufus's notes, won't we?" Hardy was not sure if his mother was making polite conversation or really meant what she said. All he could think of right then was running upstairs and tearing through boxes and drawers until he located that journal, but before he could come up with an excuse to leave the table, Alice asked, "Are we ready for pie?"

Dessert was eaten while Hardy, picking at his pie, drifted in and out of attention to the warm table talk. He decided not to look at Lily Mae while they were still eating so, as soon as guests were finishing their pie, Hardy volunteered Lily Mae and himself to clear the table and wash dishes, while the adults would sit in the living room and talk a little more. Alice looked surprised but accepted his offer. When the adults were out of range and the two young explorers began cleaning up, Lily Mae whispered in her characteristically husky voice, "Since when do you wash dishes?"

Hardy ignored her question. "You heard what Maddy said! We're onto something! The cemetery could be the key to finding out about Cherokee Ben and the early settlers! We've gotta get back out there and look at the rest of the headstones! Anyway," he paused at the kitchen sink, "who are the Moravians, and what's the Trail of Tears?"

Lily Mae finished scraping off the serving dishes. "Well, I guess you got no way o' knowin', since things like this ain't likely to be talked about at school." She began filling one side of the sink with hot water, adding some dish soap as Hardy stacked the plates and collected the silverware. Hardy could tell she was getting ready to say something important. "My grandmama told me 'bout the Trail o' Tears. The Cherokee had their own country and laws and such. The white settlers wanted their land and what was in it. The President finally sent soldiers down to take all the Cherokee to Oklahoma. A whole bunch of 'em died, 'cuz they had to walk a long way in the winter. That's why the Cherokee call it the Trail o' Tears."

By the time Lily Mae finished talking, Hardy's hands were in warm dishwater. He got really still, absently moving a dishcloth against a plate, staring at the kitchen window sill. Lily Mae was putting leftovers into the refrigerator when Hardy turned partly in her direction. "Do you think my mom knows about any of this?" Then the big idea hit him. "No! Lily Mae!" He spun around so quickly that dishwater followed his hands out of the sink and landed on Lily Mae's dress.

"Hardly Newkirk! What has possessed you?" Lily Mae was trying to brush off the water before it all soaked in. Shocked, Hardy grabbed a hand towel off the kitchen counter and handed it to his friend, who began wiping and dabbing the towel against the wettest spots.

"I'm sorry! I didn't mean to do it!" For the moment, the embarrassed boy forgot about his exciting thoughts.

There was a slight quiver in Lily Mae's voice. "These be my Sunday go-to-meetin' clothes, and I promised my mama I'd keep 'em clean!" Hardy had a pained expression on his face, but he couldn't think of anything else he could do right then. So he blurted out, "If they need special cleaning, I'll pay for it out of my allowance!"

"Everything alright in there?" Alice's voice drifted in from the living room.

"Fine, Mom, just doin' the dishes." By now, Lily Mae was fanning the towel close to the damp spots on her dress. He had an idea that he thought would help. "Hey! If you stood by the woodstove for a few minutes, I'll bet the water would dry just fine."

Lily Mae examined the damage zone one more time and then nonchalantly laid the towel on the counter. "Let's finish the dishes. We got school tomorrow."

Hardy put his hands back in the dishwater and found the dishcloth. "I'm really sorry about the water on your dress. I'll make it up to you."

Lily Mae was standing a few feet away from him against the kitchen counter. She turned and managed a weak smile. "I know. You jus' git excited sometimes."

He passed her another glass to rinse. "Yeah, I do, but I just got to thinking about Uncle Rufus's book. Do you think he says anything about the Trail of Tears? And what about the mission? Did your grandmother say anything about it?"

The slender girl with water spots on her nice dress dried the rinse water off of a dinner plate. "Hardly, if you this all-fired up about headstones and the Trail o' Tears and some missionaries, it's time to talk to my kinfolk. They been here 'bout as long as anybody, and I know I ain't heard all their stories. If your uncle's book say the same thing, we know we got somethin'."

Hardy's eyes lit up for the umpteenth time that night. "Would you take me to meet 'em?" Just then, Alice and Mr. Hunt appeared in the kitchen entrance. Mr. Hunt had his overcoat.

Alice seemed especially cheery. "Oh, wonderful, you're done with the dishes! Thank you very much, Lily Mae, for all of your help tonight. It made a big difference! You can get your things from my room now. Mr. Hunt will run Maddy home and then pick you up."

The three of them sat in the living room and talked while Mr. Hunt was gone. Hardy wanted to go looking for Uncle Rufus's book, but he knew that his mother would not have approved. Instead, they chatted about classes at school. Hardy noticed that Lily Mae asked his mother how she was enjoying her teaching at the high school. Soon, headlight beams shot high across the living room wall, and the three who were toasting by the fire rose and headed for the front door. Hardy and Alice waved from the porch, while Mr. Hunt maneuvered the car around and drove down the winding driveway.

As Hardy turned to go back into the house, he thought he detected, out of the corner of his eye, a flicker of lights down on the road away from town. Alice had gone inside already, so Hardy turned off the porch light and closed the door from outside. Then he stood still and listened. A few moments of silence passed before a sputtering engine sound drifted up to the cabin. Soon, Hardy could make out tires rolling down the gravel on the road, accompanied by the peculiar squeaks that an old pickup makes. For the better part of a minute, these sounds slowly faded. Hearing his mother calling in the house for him, Hardy opened the door and went inside.

Chapter 9

Silent Whispers

Lily Mae's uncle lived only a few blocks from the compact, tidy house in which Lily Mae lived with her mother and grandmother. Hardy had not been back to that neighborhood in Pine Gap, except when he and Alice would drop off Lily Mae after a day of exploring in the woods. He was not used to having friends whose older relatives lived with them, but he didn't think much about it, either. Lily Mae's grandmother had a room of her own in the house, and the grandchildren acted politely to her, even obeying her when she told them to do (or not do) something. The arrangements appeared to work well.

Still, Hardy had not spent much time at all with any of Lily Mae's family. Mostly, she went with him, to his neck of the woods so to speak. Today, though, it would be different. Staring out the passenger's seat window as Alice drove, Hardy was paying little attention to the houses, yards, and people that the car was passing by. Some of the adults and children stared back at their car, with an expression on their faces that left Hardy a bit puzzled. A few of the youngest children would wave, and the soon-to-be-teenager would smile and wave back. When he did so, the children invariably looked up at the nearest adult and grinned. Seeing their pleasure left a grin on Hardy's face, too.

He knew the streets well enough now to know when Lily Mae's house was approaching. She must have been standing next to the front window, for when Alice steered the car onto the driveway, Lily Mae stepped out of the door and immediately walked to their car. Hardy joined her in the back seat and, after Alice's characteristic warm greeting, Lily Mae began to give Alice directions to her uncle's house. Hardy seemed nervous.

"When did you see her last?"

"Couple o' weeks ago."

"Does she know we're coming?"

Lily Mae turned to her questioner and tipped her head down, as though she were looking over a pair of reading glasses. "You full o' questions!"

Alice chimed in from the front seat. "Lily Mae, Hardy's been pacing around the house for the last couple of days like a new father waiting for his first baby to be born! He's really excited to have this chance to listen to your great-grandmother."

"I just want to find out more about Cherokee Ben and the Moravians," the embarrassed son replied in his own defense.

"Turn right here . . . fourth house on the left." Lily Mae was leaning forward in the seat so that Alice could hear her better. In a few more moments, Hardy's mother was parking the car against the curb and turning off the engine. Hardy looked at Lily Mae, whose gaze was fixed out the window at the front door. When it opened, a handsome man, who looked a lot like Lily Mae's mother, stepped out on the porch. He and Lily Mae exchanged waves, and the two back-seat passengers piled out of the car. Lily Mae ran and gave the man a big hug, as he kissed her on the cheek. Hardy stood by, not knowing what to do. Smiling widely, Lily Mae turned to Hardy with her arm around the man. "Hardy, this my uncle—my mama's brother. Uncle James, this be Hardy, my friend from school."

A quiet but earnest smile met Hardy, as he shook the big man's hand. "I'm very pleased to meet you, Hardy. Lily Mae's mother has told me about you." He squeezed Hardy's hand a second time. The boy turned red and stuttered a bit before returning the greeting. Uncle James kept smiling, as he looked up to see Alice approaching. While they shook hands and greeted one another, Hardy caught Lily Mae's gaze for the first time since they had driven through downtown. She was still smiling, with her arm around her uncle's waist. He turned back to Hardy and addressed him.

"Well, Hardy, I hear that you would like to listen to some of great-grandmother's stories. Is that right?"

"Yes, sir." Little did he know why, the momentarily shy boy thought to himself.

"She's feeling pretty good today, so you should enjoy sitting with her. She is in her chair in the living room and is looking forward to meeting you. Let's go in, shall we?" Uncle James turned and headed back to the house, with Lily Mae happily at his side. Alice walked with Hardy, who was feeling out of place at the moment.

"You know why you're here, don't you?" He looked over at his mother, surprised by her question.

"No, why?" Suddenly, this visit took on an air of unexpected quality. Alice put her hand on the back of Hardy's head and lightly rubbed it as they stepped on to the porch.

"Because the family respects you. Respect does not come easily, yet you have earned it—with Lily Mae and her mother, too."

Hardy stopped for a moment on the porch and looked quizzically at Alice. "But I'm just a kid."

Alice lowered her voice as they entered the house. "You're not too young to be earning the trust of others." Her hand rested on his shoulder for a moment. Hardy felt strange but not in a bad way. Maybe she's saying things like this to me because my birthday is coming up, he thought, as Lily Mae met them inside the entryway and put her hand lightly on his arm. "We here. Come meet great-grandmama."

In the far corner of the front room of the house, an elderly figure with grayish-black hair sat comfortably in a faded stuffed chair. She looked to be as old as anyone whom Hardy had ever seen face-to-face—older than his grandparents—yet her face shone with vivid delight when Lily Mae approached the chair. A floral housecoat fit loosely over her slight body, pink slippers covered her feet, and her hair was long and braided. A walker sat nearby, with a TV tray on either side of the chair's oversized arms. The trays held boxes of facial tissues, a small plate with toast crumbs, a coffee mug, a magnifying glass, a couple of paperback books, and a magazine. Eyes bright with recognition caught Hardy's attention. Lily Mae escorted Hardy in front of the chair and introduced him.

"Great-gram, this is my friend, Hardy." The frail-framed woman leaned forward, reaching up with both hands open. Hardy offered his hand, which she clasped between hers, squeezing it and shaking it at the same time.

"Another Newkirk!" She kept smiling as she looked straight into his face. "You look so much like Rufus!" Hardy looked at Lily Mae, who tipped her head and muttered back with a restrained smile, "I told ya! This be Pine Gap." Quickly, Hardy remembered his manners and replied to the old woman.

"I am very pleased to meet you, ma'am. I have been looking forward to this visit." Lily Mae had pulled up two dining-room chairs, and the two adventurers sat down next to each other. Now the pleasant matriarch could easily see them both. Hardy wanted to jump right in with asking about Cherokee Ben, but he had a feeling that such a tactic would not be polite. Lily Mae spoke first.

"How ya been feelin' the last few days, Great-gram?" His friend's way of talking with her elderly relative reminded Hardy of how impressed he was with Lily Mae's manner at dinner with Maddy. The two females chatted about school, arthritis, and other family members for a while. Uncharacteristically, Hardy sat still, at one point looking behind himself to see Alice and Uncle James talking quietly at the dining-room table. Suddenly, he heard his name called, "Young Newkirk!"

Hardy sat at attention and looked at the octogenarian. "Yes, ma'am?"

"My Miz Lily say she and you been explorin' around ol' Rufus's cabin and want to learn more stories 'bout these parts." She paused and looked at him with all the presence of mind that someone half her age might have mustered.

Hardy was caught off-guard, but only for a moment. He took a breath, glanced at Lily Mae, who was looking at him approvingly, and began. "Well, yes, my mother and I moved from Draper into the cabin just before school started. She's the new art teacher at the high school. I like to take Rusty—he's my dog—out in the woods, to be outside and see things. Well, I've been making a map of the property and finding a few old things here and there, like parts of old tools and pieces of broken pottery." He paused, struck by how attentive the old woman was and how distinguished she looked right then. Trying to figure out how to broach the subject of Cherokee Ben and the Moravians without mentioning the cemetery—at least not yet—Hardy checked for any visual cues from Lily Mae. She nodded her head slightly, as if urging him to continue. He drew another long breath and looked down at his hands.

"Anyway, I met Maddy Jones, who lives not too far from the cabin. She started telling us about a mission that was here way before Pine Gap and about the Cherokee and the Trail of Tears." He stopped again and, in his hesitation, Great-grandmother spoke up, her eyes fixed on Hardy.

"I know Maddy. My son worked for her family many years, until he died. We don't see each other much anymore. How she be?"

Hardy felt some relief that the conversation was continuing. "She seems fine. Still lives in the old cabin where she was born. She had dinner at our house the other night."

"Yes, Lily Mae told me about her lovely ev'nin' and about the dishwater." The perky woman winked at the girl, who giggled while Hardy felt embarrassed and slightly set up. Great-grandmother leaned over and patted Hardy's arm. "There now, child, th' dress be fine! What else Maddy tell you?"

It was all the question that Hardy needed. Leaning forward himself, he struggled to contain his excitement as he spoke. "She mentioned someone named Cherokee Ben. She said that he was an important person for the mission and that he hid from the soldiers, and he was a leader for the other Cherokee who hid, too." He stopped for a moment or two to get a sense of her reaction. She was waiting for him to finish, so he felt that it was time to ask The Big Question. Without further hesitation, the anxious boy almost stuttered out the words. "Wha . . . what do you know . . . about Cherokee Ben, I mean?" The two youngsters sat still, but could barely contain their anticipation of the matriarch's reply.

She sunk back once again into her familiar chair, a smile of quiet satisfaction moving across her face. The two youngsters looked at each other and then again at this old woman, the elder of her clan, as her gaze wandered off, fixing momentarily on cherished days gone by, of a world passed, of echoes fading with time. When she finally spoke, it first seemed that she was talking either to herself or to some invisible character present and known only to her. "What I know about Cherokee Ben? Ben . . . aahh . . ." As her attention slowly returned to her waiting audience, they could not possibly have prepared themselves for what she was about to say. She struck such a pose in the chair with her frail body that Hardy and Lily Mae sat up, as if standing on tiptoe.

"Children . . . Cherokee Ben be one of my ancestors . . . my great-great-grandfather, to be exact." Her words were spoken so calmly that it took several seconds before the two young explorers reacted. Hardy was first to choke out words.

"Ma'am, did you say Ben was your great-great-grandfather?"

"I did, young man!"

Hardy's eyes grew as big as saucers, his mouth as wide as a flytrap, when he heard the noble woman's reply. He couldn't get any more words out, then he remembered Lily Mae sitting next to him. As he turned toward her, she grabbed his forearm, clenched her jaw, and spoke to him under her breath. "Hardly, we have to go back!"

"Somethin' wrong, children?"

Lily Mae faced her great-grandmother and showed her an innocent smile. "Nothin' wrong, Great-gram. We jus' really excited!"

Hardy squirmed in the chair and cleared his throat. "Uh, ma'am, does anybody know where Cherokee Ben was buried?" At this question, Lily Mae squeezed Hardy's arm again, not knowing whether to smile or grimace at him.

The old woman let out a quiet sigh. "Story be he buried with the Moravians, seein's he helped 'em quite a bit."

One would have thought that her two listeners were children, yearning for a first bicycle, who walked into the living room on Christmas Day to find the bike next to the tree, with a big bow on it! They both leaned over toward the other one at the same time, so quickly that their heads bumped together with an audible crack. Both wincing, then rubbing their respective points of contact, the two explorers-turning-detectives spoke to each other in hushed tones.

"We have to go back!"

"But let's tell her first!"

"I thought this was your big secret!"

"She might know somethin' that would help us!"

"Is everything okay over there?" Hardy swung around to see his mother across the room, smiling, but with raised eyebrows. He knew he had to give her an answer that was convincing.

"Fine, Mama. We're just havin' a good time talkin'." He paused to see if it worked. Alice turned back to Uncle James, as the two adults chuckled and continued chatting. Hardy glanced at the old woman, who sat smiling, waiting for the two squirrels sitting in front of her to decide what to do next. He leaned over to Lily Mae again, "I'm gonna tell her!" His companion sat still and waited. Hardy sat up again and faced the family matriarch one more time, now speaking in a lower voice. "We think we know where he might be buried—Cherokee Ben."

He spoke too softly. "Couldn't hear ya." She leaned over, turning her head slightly and cupping one ear with her hand.

Hardy glanced back at his mother and Lily Mae's uncle, then leaned over even farther and spoke in a stage whisper. "We think we know where Cherokee Ben is buried." He sat back up in his chair, waiting for her reaction. Again the old woman leaned back, looking out the window for a second or two, then took her time speaking, once more in a calm but clear voice.

"Then you found the ol' cemetery from the mission?" They couldn't tell if she meant a statement or a question.

"I think so," he replied, trying not to appear too excited but so keyed up in that moment that he felt he could run all the way home and to the cemetery site right then.

"It be really old—no new graves for over a hundred years." She fixed her gaze once more on Hardy. "You seen names on headstones?"

"About a dozen—I've rubbed most of 'em with wax paper and crayons." He dropped his voice and looked over his shoulder again. Lily Mae sat on the edge of her chair.

The old woman paused again. "Could find Ben, too, and his wives." She looked at her two energized visitors. "You must be careful. They's secrets in those graves that some ol' timers don't want let out."

Hardy wondered if Lily Mae's heart was beating as fast as his was. "But nobody knows it's there! Just me, Lily Mae, and Maddy," then he quickly dropped his voice again, "and not anybody else—not anybody." This time, Lily Mae was the one who looked over her shoulder at the two occupied adults across the room.

The girl's oldest living relative had not drawn her gaze away from Hardy. "Rufus knew. Young Newkirk, it's no accident that his land be where it is." She stared at Hardy with such intensity right then that Lily Mae glanced over to see how Hardy was reacting.

This time, the boy's voice very nearly exploded. "His book! I've got to find his book again!" Hit by this blast, Lily Mae and her great-grandmother shook their heads and blinked a few times. Alice could be heard from the dining room table, "Young man, you're getting a little rambunctious over there."

He noticed Lily Mae's glare out of the corner of her eye. Fearing that he might give away their secret, Hardy took a deep breath. "Sorry, Mama. I'll be quiet." Lily Mae was still looking at him sideways, but he decided to speak to her anyway. "Do you think you can go out there with me today?"

Her face softened enough for her to say, "Yes," and sound just convincing enough. That was all Hardy needed to hear. He addressed her great-grandmother again. "Ma'am, thank you very much for talking with us. We're gonna go look for Ben's grave, and we will come back to tell you what we find." Lily Mae nodded silently.

Stretching out her hand, the old woman took Hardy's hand, peering into his face with her piercing black eyes. "You do just that, but be careful." She squeezed his hand, then gestured for Lily Mae, who offered her hand, too, and she squeezed them both. Her eyes glistened, and Hardy suddenly felt a tingle shoot down his neck. She leaned forward, Hardy and Lily Mae following her cue. Her words were quiet yet clear, "Rememba, the old stories keep whisperin', 'til nobody listens for them no more."

Chapter 10

Cherokee Ben

RIDING HOME IN THE back seat of the car, Hardy was as nervous as a cat with new kittens. His heel tapped staccato rhythms on the floorboard, his eyes stared blankly out the back window, and his brain registered none of the picturesque scenery of leafless trees nestling against small creek beds wandering through the passing pasture land. The boy could not wait to get back up to the cemetery, to look for Ben's grave. A chance like this, to discover a lost character in the old story of his new home, almost overwhelmed him with excitement. Trying to appear nonchalant, without giving Alice any reason to suspect his plans, was driving the adventurous young boy just about crazy!

He also was mulling over something the old woman had said. Lily Mae was sitting in the front seat, talking with Alice. This meant that he would have to wait until they arrived at the cabin before the two of them could talk over what they had heard her great-grandmother tell them. "Be careful," she had said. About what? Who else would be interested in old graves, except some local history buff? What details of Cherokee Ben's story would be of interest to anyone? Hardy decided that he couldn't answer that question until he found out more about Ben.

Their vehicle was nearing the turn off the Shot when Hardy began to plan tactics for their impending cemetery visit. Mentally, he reconstructed its layout and locations of the headstones that he already had cleaned and rubbed. This gave him a better idea of what areas were still untouched, as well as the placement of partially buried headstones that he could recall. Assuming that all existing graves roughly fit a grid pattern, Hardy calculated that it would take less than an hour to confirm the location of the rest of all headstones. If he could convince Lily Mae to help, they would finish that step earlier and have more daylight for cleaning. They would rub Cherokee Ben's stone—and any others of obvious family members—for sure. He realized they would have to return on another day to complete all the rubbings.

Rusty's barking at the top of the driveway drew Hardy's mind back to the car and its climb toward the cabin. Lily Mae had packed her outdoor clothes, at home, and when Alice stopped the car, Hardy jumped out and ran to the back door without even speaking to Rusty. Lily Mae waited for Alice, who had watched her son gallop into the house. "Hardy certainly is in a hurry to get back out in the woods."

"Yes'm," his accomplice politely replied. "Great-grandmother gave us an idea of some things to look for out there." She tried to sound casual.

"Well," his mother commented, "let's hope he doesn't break a leg before he has a chance to do that!" Lily Mae was relieved that Alice appeared to suspect nothing. The girl changed clothes in the bathroom and, by the time she emerged, Hardy had their daypacks ready and was filling their canteens with water, while Alice made a couple of peanut-butter sandwiches. Rusty sat eagerly by the back door. Hardy practically snatched the sandwiches out of Alice's hands and threw them in his daypack, seized his walking stick, and careened out the door. Lily Mae was adjusting her pack, "Wait up!"

Alice was wearing one of those mother-of-a-growing-boy expressions as Lily Mae picked up her walking stick by the back door and took a step. Alice looked at the girl and said, "Lily Mae, honey?"

She turned and looked at the boy's mother. "Yes'm?"

"Could you make sure that Hardy doesn't overdo it out there? He sure is wound up about something!"

"Yes'm, I will do my best."

"Thank you, dear, enjoy yourself!"

Lily Mae had to call down the trail a few times before she spotted Hardy standing some distance below. Rusty came back to escort her. Girl and dog still were a number of steps from Hardy before he started talking to her, as loudly as he dared, without being heard by any unknown listeners in their vicinity. "I've got a plan! But I don't think we can do it all without your help."

Catching up to him as he turned to continue down the trail, Lily Mae pulled on the arm of his jacket to slow him down. "Listen, Hardly!" The boy swung back around with a quizzical look on his face. She caught his gaze in her own. "Cherokee Ben my ancestor, and I'm gonna help. But only with the clearin'. If I find one o' them grave markers, you do the rest." She kept her gaze on him.

"Sure, that's good. I'll dig, too, until we find stones to clean. I have some fresh pieces of wax paper, once—if—we find Ben's grave." Hardy had perked up with his friend's offer. The two walked side by side as the trail allowed, not talking, except when Hardy mentioned the next turn or change in direction.

They had started the final climb in elevation when Hardy turned to Lily Mae with a big grin. "Golly! Whaddaya think about having a Cherokee in your family tree?" She could tell what he thought her answer would be.

Starting to puff just a bit with the climb, Lily Mae replied candidly, "I dunno. Figgered all my ancestors be slaves. Dunno if Ben makes it any better." She was thinking more about where her feet were going just then than Hardy's unexpected question. Her companion, though, seemed enthused by this new line of thought.

"How neat would that be! Knowin' that Ben might have walked right where we're walkin' now! That you're a part of the people who had been here already, such a long time ago! They lived off the land. They knew things we don't know—about the animals, the trees, the plants . . ." Hardy was lost in dreams of a world gone by, mechanically climbing the last leg of their route, but imagining what it must have been like before log cabins and rifles, as waves of settlers began appearing in the small valleys all around them. He almost could smell smoke from a fire ring, hear the cadence of drums beating long into the night, feel an arrow leave his fingers against the bow string.

Grunting as she tried to keep up with her daydreaming chum, Lily Mae managed enough breath to call out, "Hardly!" He stopped talking and turned around, offering her a hand for the last few uneven steps. Once they were both standing on a small, level spot, Lily Mae spoke again. "You forgot somethin', boy? They's all gone! Ain't no tribes runnin' 'round these hills no more. Their way of life," she mustered enough energy to throw her hand in the air, "taken away." Almost out of breath, Lily Mae paused while the boy who had gotten her involved in his hunt for the past stood still for once, a furrowed brow screwed on his face. Straightening up after having propped herself momentarily with her hands on her thighs, Lily Mae swallowed with a dry mouth, sensing that Hardy was still listening.

"Hardly, 'bout all that's left be stories. I wanna find Ben so my great-gram knows this story don't die with her." She swallowed again, to moisten her dry mouth. Hardy kept quiet for a moment longer, gazing down at nothing in particular. When he finally spoke, his voice was softer than usual.

"Me, too." His eyes remained lowered, as though he were trying to solve a puzzle drawn on the ground in front of them. His next words came slowly, measured out, as Hardy lifted his head. "I guess I've been so excited since talking to your great-grandmother this morning that I didn't realize what all this must mean to you." When he finally looked her in the eye, he did not expect to see Lily Mae's lip quivering. He didn't know what to do next. Lily Mae didn't make him wait.

"All our stories be hidden, all o' 'em! Nobody out there," she flung her arm out wide, as though gesturing to a huge audience, "really wants to know they happened! Maybe," she took a quick breath, "maybe this one won't have to stay that way!" The girl's fists were clenched. Hardy could tell that she was about ready to cry and was caught off-guard by her own emotions. Lily Mae turned away from him and began sobbing softly, holding a fist to her mouth. It was Hardy's turn to swallow dry. Without giving it a second thought, he reached out a hand and touched her shoulder gently.

"It's okay, it's okay. If Ben's grave is here, we're gonna find it, and then we'll tell your great-grandmother and anyone else who will listen! And we'll keep lookin' 'til we find out as much as we can!" His hand had stayed on her shoulder, and it squeezed with emphasis as Hardy spoke. Suddenly, Lily Mae turned around, head still shaking with sobs, now both fists against her face, and leaned toward Hardy. He put his arms around her and patted her on the shoulders as she sobbed even harder. The boy stood, holding her gingerly, his eyes darting back and forth at nothing, hoping that Lily Mae didn't notice how intensely his heart was beating.

Gradually her sobs quieted, and after a few more moments, she leaned away from him. Hardy dropped his arms and exhaled, taking a step back while she began to sniff, rub her nose, and wipe tears from her cheeks. Then she took a big breath and straightened out her hair and jacket. Without looking up, she started walking in the direction of the cemetery, mumbling barely loud enough to be heard, "Okay, let's go." Hardy turned and followed her up the final part of the crest, as the freshly cleaned headstones slowly began to appear on the near horizon.

When they had reached the cemetery's closest boundary, Lily Mae stared ahead and asked, "Where we start?" Hardy had to stop and think about the map that he had put together in his mind while they were driving home. She was pulling off her daypack and digging around in it for the trowel that she had used last time. Hardy pulled out one of his notebooks and sketched the layout before them with a stubby pencil. Rusty already had trotted to the far end of the area and was checking for fresh scents. "Let's start with the rocks sticking out that look like they could be headstones. It shouldn't take long to get a look at each one of them."

"Where you want me?" Lily Mae spoke softly again. Her face still looked blank. Hardy walked into the center of the yard, checked a few locations, and pointed to one of the larger rocks protruding from the shaggy, uneven turf. "I guess that one is as good as any. I'll go over here," he pointed opposite her location, "and we'll work toward each other. Do you see the others to check?" He looked up at her face, since she was unusually quiet. His friend nodded, so Hardy walked over to his selected stone and began digging it out.

After an hour or so, all the stones that had been partially visible were cleared enough to read. Both explorers reviewed all these new stones, but no names, dates, or other marks on any of them suggested Cherokee Ben or his family. Hardy wished that he had time right then to get down all of the details written on each one. He stood up, wiping his brow with a forearm and looking up in the sky for the sun's position. "Looks like we have about three hours before the light starts getting dim." He dug out the peanut-butter sandwiches and walked one over to Lily Mae, who took it and thanked him. As they chewed, Hardy studied the open spaces left in the grid that slowly was appearing from their labors. Then he turned to Lily Mae and started gesturing here and there.

"We have uncovered about half of the stones, I think. Most of 'em stood upright. We've found a few that lay flat on the ground. Those are harder to read now, 'cuz the weather has worn them down more than the others." Lily Mae had walked over and was standing next to him as he pointed to various places where they had been working. He paused for a few moments, as they both studied their work site. Then Hardy looked at Lily Mae, "Do you think Ben would have a headstone that sits up or lays flat?"

Lily Mae wiped some dirt off her gloves. Her face looked more relaxed, as she thought about Hardy's question. "Flat," she finally said. "Other ones cost more. Ben's be simple." She turned to see Hardy's response.

Pulling down on his cap, the boy pursed his lips. "I think you're right. So . . . ," he reviewed the remaining open areas, honing in on the largest one, "let's start over there. If any of his family is here, they would take up some space, too." Lily Mae smiled for the first time since they had left the cabin for the trail. Pulling his trowel out of a back pocket, Hardy walked over to the selected spot and began looking for any signs of uneven or disturbed turf. He squatted down at one spot, then pointed several feet to his right. "How about you work over there. We're hopin' to find a family plot!" Lily Mae complied, and the two commenced digging.

Both explorers were using their own methods of location, but it was Lily Mae who quickly found what looked like the edge of a promising stone. Once Hardy saw it, he looked at the other stones already uncovered, made some perpendicular lines in the air with his hands, and moved his digging up and slightly closer to Lily Mae. By the time that his trowel and stick had hit a possible stone, Lily Mae was digging so fast that he could hear the trowel scraping on a larger object.

"Hardly! I got one here!" The tall girl leaned over on her knees, holding the trowel in both hands, pushing turf filled with wild grass, weeds, and tree saplings off one spot as fast as she could. A flat stone was coming into view a few inches under the surface. Lily Mae could tell that it had beveled edges, even though one end had sunk a little lower in the ground than the other end. The bottom right corner was visible, then the top right. It took only a few more seconds for the excited young lady to detect recessed carving as she moved left across the tilted surface of the headstone. "Somethin' on it!"

Her companion was listening, but he didn't move. Just a few seconds behind Lily Mae's progress, Hardy also was uncovering a flat headstone. Its features appeared identical to those that Lily Mae was finding, although neither one knew yet about the other. Right then, the two looked like they were in a contest to see who could uncover and read their stones first. "I see letters!" Lily Mae shouted out her latest discovery, as Hardy frantically scraped and shoveled.

"So do I!" By this time the boy was breathing heavily from the exertion. Lily Mae was, too, but both were so intent on their work that nothing distracted them. She had found the bottom bevel line and was moving across the stone lengthwise and right to left, trying to make out the letters. "R . . . , E . . . , T . . . , H!" Hardy was convinced that he would find words, too, once he could clear out the fine soil that stuck in the stone's cracks and crevices. But Lily Mae's discovery wouldn't wait.

"DAUGHTER! Somebody's daughter buried here!" Lily Mae did not even look up. She knew that the name and dates had to be above the word that she just cleared off. Scraping feverishly in that direction, a drop of perspiration ran down her nose. Hardy looked up long enough to see that his companion, initially unwilling to have much contact with these headstones, was working as hard as he was on them. She shouted out to him, "What you got over there?"

Hardy bent over again and returned to his scraping. "N . . . , A . . . , M . . . , MAN." Seeing that this three-letter word was located near the bottom right edge of the stone, Hardy was sure that there were other words to its left. By the time he had uncovered the next word, "FAMILY," Lily Mae called for him.

"Hardly! Come see!" The young adventurer jumped up and scrambled over to where Lily Mae was crouching. There, neatly cleaned off, visible to the world for the first time in decades, was another one of the flat headstones in the cemetery. This one, however, seemed different. Side by side, without a cue, the two excited amateurs read the stone aloud, "CHARITY CLARK, 1842–1896, DAUGHTER."

"Her parents have to be around here somewhere!" Hardy looked at Lily Mae, as they stood quietly for a few moments, trying to think. Then Hardy jumped up, startling Lily Mae. Pointing to the partially uncovered stone, he shouted, "This stone says, 'FAMILY MAN.' It's gotta be her dad!" Leaping back, the boy's hands almost shook as he carefully worked the trowel sideways, pushing years of accumulated soil and growth from the middle of the headstone. Lily Mae stood over him, watching for more letters to emerge. Above the word "FAMILY" appeared "–1877," to the left appeared "CHRISTIAN," above the date was the name "CLARK." "It's her father, all right!" Hardy could not have worked any faster. His hands were a blur of movement.

He scraped so fast and hard that the rest of the turf was cleared off in seconds. Sunlight was beginning to angle through the trees, as Hardy's companion knelt next to him while he wiped away the last layer of fine, dense soil covering the remaining characters that had been carved on that stone long ago. Hardy was too determined to finish quickly that he was not reading as he went. Then, quite before he realized it, the job was done. The headstone was cleared and cleaned, about twenty inches long and nine inches tall. Bending over first to blow the last bits of finest soil off the surface, Hardy sat up, looked at the stone, and grabbed Lily Mae's arm.

A low whistle left his lips. The two diggers stared at each other, groping for words. Hardy looked back at the stone, then back again at Lily Mae. "Holy cow! We did it! We did it!" He squeezed her arm.

Lily Mae sat on her knees, in a trance. "Sweet Jesus, there he be . . . just like Great-gram say." Her eyes glassed up as she remained motionless, gaping at the words of the headstone in front of them. Sensing her mood, Hardy read the inscription aloud, as solemnly as he could muster, "BENJAMIN CLARK, 1795?–1877, CHIEF, CHRISTIAN, FAMILY MAN."

Neither one of them moved or spoke. Rusty walked up and sat down on the other side of the headstone from his master. A shaft of low sunlight hit the stone and moved across it slowly, as if punctuating the occasion. It was a moment unlike any other that either youngster ever had known.

"Where's her mama?" Lily Mae's sudden question broke the aura of magnificence in an instant. Hardy blinked.

"What?"

"Charity's mama. She would o' been married to Ben. She would o' been a slave. Musta run away, unless Ben bought her."

Hardy had not been thinking along those lines. He pulled a dry one-inch paint brush out of his pack and started preparing the stone for a crayon rubbing. "Well," he replied nonchalantly, "if the daughter is on that side, then," he pointed to a flat, untested location opposite, "I'll bet the mother is right there."

That was all Lily Mae needed to hear. While Hardy spread out the wax paper over Ben's headstone, the long-dead man's young descendant picked up her trowel and headed for the spot to which Hardy pointed. As he rubbed Ben's stone carefully with a black crayon, she began probing the spot for a hard surface below the turf line. Hardy was still rubbing when Lily Mae had located another stone. He had to hold the wax paper in place on Ben's stone, while she cleared the new find by herself. In a couple of minutes, the inscription was clear; Lily Mae's hunch proved correct. She read aloud while Hardy finished Ben's rubbing, "ABIGAIL CLARK, 1825?–1881, WIFE."

Standing up while still studying the inscription, Lily Mae took a deep breath and exhaled, as though a weight had been lifted. She turned to Hardy, who was rolling up the rubbing to store in his daypack for the trip back to the cabin. "Rub these two, please?" Her two index fingers were pointing to the women's headstones, on either side of Ben's.

Hardy pulled out more wax paper. "I wasn't planning on it, but we have just enough time right now. It will go faster, if you help hold the paper in place. Then we'll still be able to go by and see if Maddy is home. I think she wants to know. Remember how mysterious she acted at dinner?"

Lily Mae bent over the nearest stone and waited for Hardy to lay the piece of wax paper across it. "She knowed already you was up here," the girl mused. It took only a few minutes each, and both rubbings were finished. Placing them carefully in a pocket of his daypack, Hardy looked around to make sure they had picked up everything they had brought with them. He checked the angle of the sun once more.

"We have enough time to make it to Maddy's, talk to her a little, then get back to the cabin before it gets dark." As usual, Rusty had figured out what was happening and had begun to pick out a descent route. The two triumphant explorers followed, moving quietly, their minds filled with their new discoveries. By now, Hardy knew the way to Maddy's from the cemetery, without consulting his hand-drawn maps. Most of the hike was easy. The air still felt comfortable for a November afternoon, and the bare trees allowed light to linger longer.

Before they reached the "No Trespassing" sign, the youngsters could hear activity coming from the direction of Maddy's cabin. Hardy thought it sounded like firewood being thrown onto a pile. He turned to Lily Mae, "Looks like Maddy has company." Hearing his words, she slowed down at the fence and hesitated to crawl through it. Surprised that she stopped, Hardy gave her a puzzled look. Her voice dropped.

"Maddy like me, but don't think her kinfolk do."

The boy was feeling self-assured, but he saw the look on her face. "Well, okay," he paused, "then how about if we sneak over to the edge of the clearing and wait for a while, to see if her visitor leaves soon? We've come this far, and it would be another week before we can go see her together. I don't know if I can wait that long!"

Lily Mae sighed. "As long as we be quiet." She bent over to straddle through the old barbed-wire fence and noticed that Rusty was on the other side already. "What about the dog? Will he bark?" She looked nervously at the dog's master.

"Rusty! Heel!" The dog trotted back to the boy and stayed at his side as they began picking their way through the undergrowth. Lily Mae watched for a moment and then followed. The thumping of split wood being tossed and landing on a pile got louder and then stopped. Voices near the cabin began speaking, and Maddy's two young friends walked more slowly, watching every step. It became clear that the old woman was talking to a man. When Hardy saw the fresh pile of firewood through the trees, he stretched out his arm, and the three stopped walking. It was hard to see Maddy and the man, but their voices got louder and became easier to understand.

"Now you know those kids ain't doin' no harm out there!"

"Aunt Maddy, they could get to meddlin', and I ain't gonna like that!"

Hardy and Lily Mae froze, and Hardy gestured for Rusty to sit. The two looked at each other with wide eyes. Lily Mae leaned over and whispered in Hardy's ear, "We shouldn't o' come!"

He turned and whispered back, "If we move now, he might hear us." Lily Mae reluctantly stood by, trying to be as still as she could.

"Now you listen to me, Junior! They's just kids havin' a good time explorin' the woods. You leave well enough alone, y'hear?"

"Them young'uns are playin' with a hornet's nest, and you know it! And what's Rufus's boy doin' runnin' 'round with a colored girl? It ain't natural, I tell ya!"

"It's a new day, Junior. The old ways don't apply no more."

"Well, I don't hafta like it, and I just might hafta do somethin' about it!"

Lily Mae was beside herself by now. Grabbing Hardy's hand, she pulled him close enough to whisper again. "I'm scared, Hardly! That man mean!"

The boy's heart had kicked into high gear again, but he didn't want Lily Mae to be any more distressed than she was feeling already. He tried to calm her down, "I think he's gonna leave in a minute; the wood's all piled now." He squeezed Lily Mae's hand and turned back to peer through the brush at the scene in the distance.

"You know how our kin take care o' things around here!"

"Junior, if you try to touch even a hair on those kids' heads, you'll have to answer to me!"

"I ain't 'fraid o' you, Aunt Maddy!"

"Now put that thing away, before ya do somethin' foolish with it! You hear me, young man?"

"Mind your own business, old woman!"

The two voices by the cabin suddenly got muffled, and Hardy could feel Lily Mae shivering. Straining to see through the brush, Hardy tried to make out what was going on in the distance. Then, without warning, near the old cabin's back door he saw a tiny flash of light and a puff of smoke. A split-second later the two scared kids heard the popping sound of a pistol. Lily Mae screamed; without thinking, Hardy cupped his hand over her mouth. Rusty barked and stood up, as another sound, this one of an old truck engine turning over, drifted across the clearing and into the woods. Hardy thought he could see the truck moving across the clearing and around the house. He removed his hand from Lily Mae's mouth, while Rusty ran toward Maddy's cabin, barking. Then Hardy remembered where he had heard that truck sound before.

Chapter 11

Robes

"He shot Maddy!" Lily Mae screamed again, and this time Hardy knew it was useless to try to stop her. Rusty's barking was coming from the same direction as the shot that was fired. "Come on!" Lily Mae was tugging on Hardy's hand. "We gots ta help Maddy!" She let go of his hand and started moving through the brush as fast as she could get through it. Hardy took off behind her, trying to see if the truck was out of sight and earshot by then. By the time they reached the edge of the clearing, they could see Maddy lying on the ground next to her porch, as still as death.

"Maddy, Maddy, you awright?" Lily Mae was shouting even before she got close to the prostrate body. She reached the old woman and was puffing for breath as she bent over next to her head. "Maddy, you hear me?" Hardy caught up and knelt down next to his friend, who was lightly slapping Maddy's cheeks. "I think she unconscious. Where's she shot?"

Hardy looked at Maddy and saw a dark red spot forming on her dress and jacket, on her left side below the collarbone. "Right here." He examined it for a moment, not considering that he had never seen a gunshot wound in his life. Lily Mae was still trying to wake Maddy. Hardy looked up at the sky. "The sun is going down soon, and it's gonna get cold out here." He put a hand on Lily Mae's shoulder. "We've got to get her inside. Can you hold her legs if I pick her up under the arms?"

"She still bleedin'!"

Hardy was trying to think fast. "Run into the kitchen and see if you can find a towel or somethin' that we can wrap around her chest. Maybe that will slow it down 'til we get her inside." Lily Mae jumped up and ran across the porch and into the cabin. Hardy tried to get a pulse from Maddy's wrist but finally found it on her neck. It was rapid and shallow. Lily Mae returned with a thin, stained kitchen towel, but it was long enough. Hardy lifted Maddy's left shoulder a few inches off the ground so that Lily Mae could pull one end of the towel under the unconscious woman's left armpit. She then brought the other end around the opposite side of Maddy's neck, tying the two ends right over the wound. Hardy had rummaged through his pack and found a spare pair of socks, which Lily Mae used as a gauze pad.

"I guess that'll have to do. The sooner we get her in the house, the sooner we can stop the bleeding." Hardy stood up, breathing deeply, and looked down at the motionless woman. "Maybe it would work better for me to take one arm and you to take the other." Lily Mae was listening. "We just won't pull hard." Hardy put his hands under Maddy's left armpit, while Lily Mae did the same with the right. Huffing and grunting, they lifted the woman off her back and gingerly dragged her toward the porch. One of her shoes came off, but they kept pulling her, slowly taking the rickety steps one at a time, keeping her back suspended in the air. Once inside the house, Hardy kicked the door closed with his foot. He could tell that Maddy had kept a fire going in her stove earlier in the day. He saw a kettle sitting on top and hoped that there was some warm water in it.

Dragging her between the stove and the kitchen table, Maddy's two young friends laid her down as gently as they could. Removing their packs, Hardy shoved them under the kitchen counter, out of the way. Then he ran into the other room—the one that he had seen through a doorway on an earlier visit—and came back a few moments later with a couple of blankets. As he rolled Maddy to one side, Lily Mae positioned one blanket under the pale woman. As he covered her with the second blanket, he felt her hands and checked her pulse again. She was cool to the touch. Her pulse was getting faint and her breathing shallow. Lily Mae had picked up the kettle and was looking for a clean bowl. "Is there warm water in it?" Hardy asked.

"Uh-huh," Lily Mae replied, quickly lifting a ceramic bowl from a shelf near the sink, wiping it out with a dry dishcloth, and pouring in the hot water. "I'll clean off the blood and see if the bleedin' will stop." Hardy was still kneeling by Maddy. He looked up at his friend, who had been crying earlier in the day and now was taking charge of Maddy's first aid. Staring at the floor for a moment, he threw his hands up in the air, "What should I do now?"

Lily Mae was facing the kitchen counter, gathering the makeshift cleaning supplies. "Go get help." Hardy didn't move or speak. Lily Mae picked up the bowl and turned to place it next to Maddy. She looked squarely into

Hardy's eyes. "Got to call an amb'lance . . . your house th' closest one with a phone. Go . . . now! Got to get her to a hospital!" She set the bowl on the floor near the woman's elbow and turned to gather the clean rags.

Hardy didn't move or even blink. Lily Mae was back at Maddy's side with the rags, lifting the damaged side of the dingy jacket away from the bullet's entry point. "Now, Hardly, now!" The boy opened his mouth to speak, raising his hand for emphasis. Lily Mae gave him one of her fierce looks. "Boy, what part of 'Go' don't ya understand? Maddy needs a doctor! Get goin'!"

As if finally waking up, Hardy sprang over to his pack, rustled through it until he found a flashlight and a whistle. Checking the flashlight for beam strength, he handed the whistle to Lily Mae. "What this for?"

"Here. Put this in your pocket. If anything happens, blow it as hard as you can, and I'll come for you."

"Hardly! Please get goin'!"

Rusty was waiting on the porch as Hardy opened the back door. He turned on the flashlight and looked at Lily Mae one more time. "Don't forget the whistle!"

"Got it!" Hardy caught a glimpse of the red stain all over the front of Maddy's dress as he left the cabin. Rusty barked and ran toward the edge of the clearing. Hardy aimed the flashlight at his canine companion and took long strides to the brush line. The sun was going down, and dark shadowy patches began appearing everywhere. He looked for anything he could use to get his bearings and wished that he had kept his compass in his jeans pocket. Rusty, however, seemed to know where to go. He stayed not too far ahead of his master, keeping a steady pace through the brush.

Gingerly easing himself through the rusty barbed-wire fence, Hardy knew then that it would take only a few more minutes to reach the main trail. Once he got there, he figured he could jog the rest of the way, even if it wore him out. His mother would call the ambulance, and then the two of them could scramble back to Maddy's to help Lily Mae. Having to follow Rusty through the graying forest, with its abundance of large, gaunt, creepy shapes all around him, was giving Hardy the shivers. He kept the flashlight beam aimed in Rusty's direction and talked to the dog, to keep his mind off the places where his imagination could have taken him right then.

Somewhere up ahead, Rusty was barking rather regularly, but the sound was starting to echo a little, and Hardy was having a hard time finding the dog with his flashlight. Breathing hard already, the boy began to worry that he couldn't jog the final stretch up to their cabin. He called a little louder to the trailblazing dog, "Rusty! Hold on, boy. Let me catch up, 'til we get to the main trail!"

His canine pal must have stopped for a moment, for Hardy heard no barking. He aimed the flashlight in the direction of the dog's last yelp, and he thought he saw a turn into the main trail, up ahead. "I'm comin', boy! Good dog!" The tired boy breathed a small sigh of relief and took steps toward that turn. Then, without any warning, Hardy suddenly found himself being squeezed around the middle and lifted off the ground. He yelled out in surprise, aware that he was moving, his feet dangling in the air, suspended by a tight grip on his rib cage.

"What are you doing?" the boy screamed, shocked and frightened. His arms stuck up in the air awkwardly, but he couldn't move them. He kicked his feet back and forth, making contact with something behind them that seemed to be moving. A moment later, a smooth fabric surface brushed quickly across one side of his face, followed by a heavy thud against his temple. "Ow! That hurt!" Then Hardy realized that he could feel warm, heavy breath against the back of his neck. "Who are you? What do you want?" His heart was beating fast, his mind moving even faster.

Hardy could not tell how long he was carried nor in which direction he was going. Dusk had settled on the forest, to the point that he could see nothing. He didn't know where his flashlight had gone. After his cries, questions, and gyrations got him nowhere, he decided to hold still and listen for clues. A large person—he figured it must be a man—held him in a bear hug and was breathing down his neck. Every time his captor took a step, Hardy could hear the swishing sound of fabric pieces rubbing together. He thought he could make out a gurgling sound getting louder.

Then, abruptly, he landed hard on the ground, with a breath-shaking thud. Now the gurgling sound was close, right next to his head. Gasping for breath, he looked up, just as a bright light shone onto his face, leaving him squinting blindly. For the first time, a voice spoke, gruff and middle-aged, "Boy, you better stay outta things that ain't your business, understand?"

Hardy tried to speak. His lips moved, but no words came out of his mouth. Then, he heard Rusty barking, off in the distance. "Rusty! Rusty!" As he yelled, the large figure holding the bright flashlight turned slightly in the direction of the dog's barking. Immediately, it turned back again, and Hardy heard the menacing voice again. "You hear me, boy?" In the space of a half-second, the shivering lad on the ground caught a glimpse of a large, flowing, white blur, swishing with the figure's movement. Before he had a chance to get a better look, though, Hardy felt a penetrating pain on the side of his head, one so harsh that he couldn't breathe again. He was fading out as that same voice grumbled, "Where is that cussed animal?" A few moments later, he heard several shots up the trail. Then everything went black.

Blue-black darkness, cold, throbbing, no sound except a loud and constant splash and burble, dream-like images, and woozy sounds floated all around the young adventurer. He laid still for a long time, moaning softly now and then, watching Rusty run down the trail and then back again, hearing Lily Mae telling him it was time to get up and go. He wanted to move, but it seemed too hard. All he knew was darkness, cold, throbbing, splash, and burbling.

Then he heard Rusty barking. Hardy tried to speak his name, but he had no energy to form words. The barking was getting louder. With effort, the boy tried to move his arms to push himself off the ground. Suddenly he realized that his hand was resting in cold, moving water. Tingling from the sudden temperature change, he realized how much his head hurt. His other hand dragged up to the throbbing area, where he felt a lump the size of an egg, with a small sticky spot in the middle. Hardy winced, finally aware that he was no longer dreaming.

Rusty's bark got even louder. Hardy opened his mouth and croaked out a feeble, scratchy, unearthly sound. He thought he could hear grass and bushes rustling. In a few more moments, he felt licking on his head. "Rusty!" he whispered hoarsely, as the dog licked and nuzzled the injured boy's face. Rusty paused his nursing gesture and barked a few times. Hardy laid still and let Rusty's presence comfort him. After a few more moments, above the sounds of the creek, Hardy thought he could hear voices.

With the one eye that would open, he looked out into the dark and thought he saw a pin-sized light bobbing back and forth. Voices got louder, and Rusty barked again. By then, Hardy could hear his mother talking. She sounded very distressed. Who was with her, he wondered, as he tried to shake off his stupor. The light became larger and brighter. "I see Rusty!" Then the beam fell across Hardy's body. "My God, Richard, Hardy's hurt!"

Hearing his mother's voice, Hardy tried to stand. All he could do, however, was make a frail attempt to sit up; he was too dizzy. Alice rushed over to him, as Mr. Hunt held the flashlight for her to see. Rusty sat by his master, as Alice squatted down and threw her arms around Hardy's neck. Her words tumbled over each other.

"Oh, my baby! What happened? When Rusty came back to the cabin without you, I just knew something was wrong. It was almost dark. Thank goodness Mr. Hunt had come over for a visit! Honey, your head! We have to get you to the hospital! Where's your pack?" Hardy was too weak to try to interrupt Alice's torrent of anxious words. She hugged him, looked at his face, hugged him again, began checking for other possible wounds, and hugged him once more. Suddenly, her head shot back and up, as though she were hit by a bolt of lightning. Alice looked around the vicinity for a split second. "Hardy! Where is Lily Mae?"

Mr. Hunt leaned over as the boy swallowed, took a slow breath, and began to recount the incident in a soft, gravelly voice. "Mama, we went to tell Maddy what we found today, and there was a man there unloading firewood. He finished, and they got into an argument, and he shot her. Lily Mae stayed with Maddy, so I could run back to our cabin and call an ambulance."

Alice paused and, in the dark forest, Hardy could not see the fear that crept across her face. "Did the same man do this to you? What did he want?"

Standing up quickly, Mr. Hunt spoke solemnly, "We've got to get to Maddy's as soon as we can. Hardy, are you able to walk? How far is it to Maddy's from here?"

Alice balanced her son while he tottered to his feet. "In the dark, it'll take about ten minutes, if we don't get lost. Rusty should know the way."

"Son," Alice got quiet. "How bad is Maddy?"

"The bullet went right here," he pointed to his chest, "and we couldn't wake her up. Her pulse was weak when I left." Hardy's head pounded, his vision was still a little blurred, and he kept his arm on his mother's shoulder.

"Maybe I should go with Rusty to Maddy's by myself. Then, the two of you could call an ambulance and get Hardy checked out." Mr. Hunt was trying to come up with the best action plan.

"I'm not leaving my friend again! She was taking really good care of Maddy when I left!" Hardy felt a surge of energy now. "I can't leave her! It's my fault all this happened!"

"Honey, you're injured! It might be too much for you, and someone has to call an ambulance for Maddy, as soon as possible!"

Hardy started to object when Mr. Hunt interrupted, "I guess my idea wasn't a good one." He looked out into brush and trees that now were eerily pitch black. "It's probably better that we stay together."

"Rusty, let's go to Maddy's house!" Hardy's head hurt, and he wobbled as he tried to stay on his feet, but he was ready to move. The dog barked and trotted off. Mr. Hunt aimed the flashlight where the dog was heading, and the three of them followed. Alice kept a hand on Hardy's arm. She wanted to hear what happened to her inquisitive son, but it was too hard to talk, as they made their way among brambles with only one flashlight. Rusty was earning his keep, getting the trio to the barbed-wire fence in just a few minutes. Woodstove smoke hung faintly in the air, but Hardy thought he could see light from the cabin's lamps by then.

When they were approaching the edge of the clearing, Hardy called out Lily Mae's name. There was no answer. He called again but heard nothing back. Rusty barked and trotted into the clearing. It was then that Hardy saw the back door ajar. He didn't understand why Lily Mae would leave it open to the night air. Then a chill ran down his spine, as he remembered what her great-grandmother had said.

"Something's wrong!" The boy broke away from his mother's hold and hobbled as quickly as he could through the brush to the clearing. Alice and Mr. Hunt picked up their pace as well, watching Hardy's silhouette cross the clearing to the porch. He called out the girl's name once more, as he stiffly hobbled up the porch steps and pushed the door all the way open. Alice could see Hardy disappear into the cabin, and she ran in the dim light to the porch. When she got inside, she saw Maddy on the floor, motionless, but no one else in sight. A rustling sound in the next room startled the panicked mother, until her son appeared at its door.

His face told the story. "She's not here! Lily Mae's gone!" Mr. Hunt was in the cabin by now and immediately checked on Maddy, whose chest was covered with blood. The makeshift bandage was also crimson. "She wouldn't leave Maddy!" Hardy was beginning to hyperventilate, as Alice was trying to calm him down and also pay attention to what Mr. Hunt would say about Maddy's condition. Hardy began to cry. "It's all my fault! Now she's in trouble, big trouble!"

The quiet teacher looked up at the frantic boy and his distraught mother. "If there's any life left in her, it's barely hanging on." He looked at Hardy. "Maddy doesn't drive any more, but does she have a car?"

Hardy took a deep breath, then pointed to the opposite side of the house. "I saw an old pickup sitting out there, once." He sniffed, wiping tears off his cheeks with a dirty jacket sleeve.

Mr. Hunt looked somberly at the boy's mother, then started checking around the room for something. "Alice, if I can get that truck started, I'm driving Maddy to the hospital. Have you ever shot a gun? I want you to look for a pistol or something right now, to take with you back to your place. Aim the flashlight low to the ground, keep Rusty quiet, and don't talk! Get in your house, lock the doors, and call the sheriff. Tell him that I have a dying woman in an old pickup and am heading to the hospital!" He turned back to look at her and found both mother and son staring at him with disbelief. "Do you understand everything I have said?"

"Yes, Richard, but . . . "

"There's no time to explain!" The calm teacher's eye caught a glint hanging from a nail in the wall. He walked briskly to retrieve a key ring, inspecting it long enough to see what he wanted. "Here's the key to the truck. Maddy might have kept a pistol in her bedroom. See if you can find it." Taking the flashlight, Mr. Hunt ran out the door. In a few moments, Alice and Hardy could hear the truck's starter turning over, as they scoured Maddy's bedroom. Hardy lifted up the top corner of the mattress and, sure enough, he found her pistol there, just as they heard the truck engine fire up. Mr. Hunt held the throttle high for several seconds to ensure that the engine would keep running. Then he bounded back up the porch steps and into the cabin, setting the flashlight on the kitchen counter.

Hardy had given Alice the pistol. Her hands shook as she opened the chamber to check for bullets. Mr. Hunt saw the gun, as he eased Maddy off the floor, dragging her the same way that the two scared youngsters had done at dusk. From the doorway, he hoisted Maddy onto one shoulder and looked back at the other two. "Before you leave, see if she has any more ammunition. And, then, get going! Stay in your cabin until you hear from me!" He disappeared down the rickety steps, with Maddy's limp body hanging over his shoulder, like a rag doll.

Alice stood motionless for a moment, then closed the pistol chamber. "Hardy, where would Maddy keep more bullets for this gun?" With a throbbing head, the boy thought for a moment and returned to Maddy's bedroom. Alice tried to clean up some of the blood on the floor. Hardy returned with a box.

"How many should I get out?" He fingered the lid nervously.

"Good Lord, just dump a bunch in your jacket pocket and put the box back. Did you turn out the lamp in there?"

"I will." Hardy did as she said and was ready to go in a moment. Before walking out the door, he remembered that both he and Lily Mae had taken off their daypacks when they got Maddy inside. For a split second, his heart sank, thinking that Lily Mae's kidnapper had stolen their packs, along with all of Hardy's drawings and rubbings of the day. A moment later, he was relieved to see both of them sitting under the kitchen counter, right where he had tossed them. They must have been out of sight enough for the intruder not to notice them. Starting to shiver from the night air, the boy bent over to pick up the two packs and handed Lily Mae's to his mother.

Alice gave Hardy the flashlight, turned out the two kerosene lamps in the kitchen, and stuck the pistol in her coat pocket. "Mama, have you ever shot a gun before?"

"Not since you were born." She opened the door and they walked off the small porch to a waiting Rusty. Outside, the blackest of dark nights enveloped them. The flashlight poked only a tiny hole in the seemingly fathomless gloom all around them. As they crossed the clearing, Hardy asked his mother, "What will you do, if you see somebody bad in the forest?"

Alice drew a determined breath. "Son, right now, all I have to do is to think of what has happened tonight to your lovely friend, and I will do what needs to be done." She paused. "Tell me what happened to you."

Hardy hesitated. So much had taken place that day. He couldn't decide who needed to know what. "I guess it was a big man. He grabbed me from behind and carried me over to that creek and threw me down, and then I guess he kicked me in the head."

Alice's voice trembled a little. "Could you see him?"

"Not really, but it felt like he was wearing a big, loose robe or something. I got a little look at it before I passed out. I was afraid that he shot Rusty!" He stopped talking, suddenly, and Alice could tell that he had something else on his mind.

"What else do you need to tell me, honey?" Looking up a moment to check on Rusty's path, Alice put her arm through her son's.

Hardy felt hot tears on his cheeks. "I . . . I'm afraid . . . afraid that the same man went back and kidnapped Lily Mae!"

Chapter 12

The Search

WALKING HOME AT NIGHT in Draper had never bothered Hardy. The streets in their neighborhood were quiet, with enough light from street lamps and front porches to make it easy to see where you were going. Even though he had spent the first few months in Pine Gap joyfully traipsing through these woods and hills, the walk back to the cabin that night with Alice felt very different. He never realized how utterly incomprehensible nighttime could be, with a tree canopy that camouflaged the sky and stars, uneven terrain that could fool you from one step to the next, sounds magnified and menacing by the lack of any other clear sensory input, and images that thrust themselves in your way, made ghoulish by dim artificial light. For the first time that he could remember, darkness left Hardy feeling nervous.

Surely his apprehensions had something to do with the immediate circumstances. Maddy had been shot at her cabin and was unconscious, Hardy had been roughed up at dusk by a stranger and dumped in the woods, and no one knew what had happened to Lily Mae! The nights in late summer, when Hardy and Alice had sat out by the swing and watched for shooting stars, seemed, at the time, to offer a respite of wonder and peace. Now, as mother and son trudged as quietly as they could to find the trail and get home to call the sheriff, night was revealing yet another side of itself to the boy who loved the outdoors.

Alice was keeping her right hand inside the pocket that was holding the pistol. She and Hardy walked as close together as they could manage under the conditions, following the flashlight beam that Hardy held barely a few feet in front of them. Rusty seemed to sense that something was up and walked only a couple of lengths ahead, sniffing loudly, with ears cocked forward. In spite of their attention to where they stepped, inevitably a twig got snapped now and then, leaving the two checking with each other through gestures and quiet whispers that everything was okay.

Once they saw the light shining from their cabin's back door, Hardy was ready to talk. Alice quickly silenced him, fearing that someone could be lurking in the shadows. As they approached the place where the trail met the clearing near the back of the house and the woodshed, Alice handed Hardy the key to the back door and then whispered in his ear. "First, see if the door is locked. If it is, go ahead and unlock it. If the door is unlocked, open it a few inches, back away, and let Rusty go in." The boy nodded and walked toward the door with as much caution as he could muster, while Alice took the pistol out of her pocket, gripping the handle, her trigger finger ready.

Hardy placed his hand on the door knob and gave it a turn. It didn't budge. He inserted the key into the lock. Alice stood next to him, with her back to the door. Rusty stood at Hardy's feet and slipped inside, as Hardy turned the knob and slowly opened the door. Alice pulled back on Hardy's arm, giving Rusty time to inspect the cabin. Then she slipped her hand just inside the door, feeling against the wall until she found the triple-switch plate. She turned on the lights for the kitchen and dining room, and the two stepped inside, gliding through the doorway, like ghosts.

Hardy gestured at Rusty to go upstairs, and the large dog obeyed the silent command. Hardy and Alice glanced around, as much as their tight vantage point allowed. When Rusty returned, Alice rushed to the phone. The county's emergency numbers were printed on a card, taped to a kitchen-cabinet door. Alice called the sheriff's number and reported Maddy's shooting, Mr. Hunt's hospital destination, Hardy's experience in the woods, and Lily Mae's disappearance.

As she spoke with the dispatcher, Hardy pulled on his mother's sleeve. "Tell them I want to go with a deputy, to look for Lily Mae!" Alice turned and put her index finger up to her lips. Then Hardy heard his mother giving the dispatcher Lily Mae's description. She turned again, "What color is her coat?" Hardy tried to answer all of the questions, before asking his mother one more time about riding along. Impatient, he remembered that he still had on his daypack. Pulling it off, the boy set it down inside the laundry room, after making sure that all of the pockets and spaces were zipped up, revealing none of their contents. Finally, Alice hung up the phone. Turning around, she sighed.

"They're sending a couple of cars out here to the house. The deputies want to talk with you, to get more details. They will use their searchlights along the roads on the way here, just in case. When they get here, you can ask about riding with one of them." Even though it was not late, his mother looked tired. As she spoke to him, Hardy's mind went back to the night that Uncle Rufus had died, and Alice had spent a lot of time on the phone. "I'm going to have to call Mrs. Nolan and tell her what has happened."

Hardy gave his mother a pleading look. "Can't we wait a little bit, to see if we can find her right away?"

Alice smiled wearily. "When you are a parent, you will understand." She looked up the number and dialed. The boy, with a throbbing head and a goose-egg bump that needed cleaning, stood next to his mother, his heart once again pounding furiously. He could tell from her statements and comments that Lily Mae's mother was quite distressed with the news. When he could not stand still anymore, he began pacing back and forth on the kitchen floor. Alice was saying her "okays" and "goodbyes" on the phone, as Hardy gripped the edge of the kitchen counter with his hands and waited. Alice hung up the phone.

"Of course, Mrs. Nolan is very upset," she began. "She has known Maddy for years." At this statement, Hardy's eyebrows shot up and he leaned forward. "She says that Maddy is a good woman, and she hopes that she will be alright." Alice stopped for a moment and began to pull off the daypack that she had worn since leaving Maddy's cabin. "As for Lily Mae, she asked if she could come here to wait. She is calling her brother James for a ride. She is also contacting their pastor, to start the prayer chain at their church." Seeing that Hardy was hanging on her every word, Alice continued. "Before everyone gets here, let's clean up your wound and eat a few leftovers."

A few minutes later, Hardy's temple sported a gauze bandage, complete with every cleanser and ointment in the first-aid kit that Alice could think of using. The boy had assisted her efforts by wincing, jerking, and otherwise protesting every time she touched the vicinity of the still-pulsating abrasion.

Washing up thoroughly, Alice then moved into the kitchen, while Hardy now had a chance to remove his boots and change out of his grimy explorer clothes. He could hear his mother talking to him through the bathroom door. "I sure am grateful for microwave ovens! What will they think of next?" He could tell that she was trying to help him relax. When he had dressed, Hardy went into the kitchen and started fidgeting with whatever was sitting on the counter.

"Why can't I take Rusty and go back out in the woods? Maybe we could find her before the sheriff's deputies get here. Wouldn't her mother be relieved!" Hoping that a short plea might work better than a long one, he stopped talking, as the bandaged goose egg on his head continued to keep time with his pulse. Alice didn't break her stride. Her hands moved almost automatically in and out of the cabinets, drawers, and refrigerator.

"Honey, it is taking every ounce of my energy to resist going back out there right now but, if the people who took Lily Mae are still around, what good will it do to have even more people for the sheriff to look for? Besides, you could have had a concussion. We haven't had a chance to get you examined so, please, feed Rusty, stoke the stove, and sit quietly until dinner is ready."

Hardy knew that was that. Tending to the fire, he sat down in the rocker for a few minutes, until Alice called him to eat. Between bites, Hardy mused aloud on directions that he thought the deputies might take to look for Lily Mae. Alice encouraged him to share those ideas when the officers arrived.

The wait was not long. Headlight beams danced eerily across the cabin's interior walls a few minutes later. Food still on his dinner plate, Hardy was standing by the door when the knock came. Two uniformed officers, wearing leather jackets, stiff-brimmed hats, boots, and large pistols in holsters, greeted Hardy. Alice was walking to the door as they stepped inside. "Have you found her yet?" The anxious boy couldn't wait.

"No signs of the missing child yet," the older-looking officer replied, in a matter-of-fact, professional tone of voice. "The dispatcher has sent out an APB to all other officers. We are here to search the immediate vicinity, since there is a good chance she was not taken far away."

Hardy jumped right in. "I'm hoping they just wanted to scare her a little, like they did to me."

The second officer spoke. "What happened to you, son? We can see the bandage on your head." He had pulled out his notepad.

Hardy took a breath and recounted the story, from the time he and Lily Mae had wiggled through the barbed-wire fence until he and Alice returned to their cabin to call the sheriff.

"And you say there was just one attacker?"

"I didn't see a second person, but it all happened so fast."

"Did you get a look at him?"

Hardy hesitated. "Not exactly. I could tell that he was a lot bigger than me. He didn't say anything until I almost had passed out. He had a drawl when he talked, and he shot a gun at Rusty!" The boy looked gratefully at his dog, lying on the floor, warming himself close to the woodstove.

"Any idea what he was wearing?"

"I could feel something big and long all around him, like a sheet. I could hear one part of the fabric swishing against another. Just before I passed out, it looked like he was wearing a ghost costume, like a huge blur of white." He paused. "The last thing I remember was wondering why this man was wearing a ghost costume, when Halloween was a couple of weeks ago."

The two officers turned their heads slightly toward each other and exchanged darting glances. Alice noticed and stared at the floor, shaking her head. Hardy was still tuned into his conversation with the officers. The older-looking one moved to a new topic.

"You know these woods pretty well?"

Adventurous as he might have felt earlier in the day, at that moment the novice mountain boy felt little confidence about anything. "Well, I guess so. I've been exploring the area between our cabin and Maddy's since before school started. I have a map mostly finished." He wondered what they would think of his hobby.

"Let's take a look at it. You can show us where Miz Jones was shot, where you were taken, where the young lady was located before she disappeared—things like that."

In spite of his worry over Maddy and Lily Mae, Hardy grinned to think that adults—and sheriff's deputies, no less!—wanted to look at one of his hand-drawn maps. Alice moved dinner things off the table, while Hardy went into the laundry room to fetch his biggest map project. Although it was not quite finished, he knew he could point out everything they needed. Unzipping the main compartment of his daypack, the top of one of his rolls of headstone rubbings popped out. Hardy shuddered and pushed it back inside, looking back over his shoulder into the kitchen. He blew out a big breath, then rummaged through the same compartment, locating the largest map and pulling it out. The officers were seated at the table, when Hardy returned. He proudly unfolded and spread his prized work out on the end of the table.

For several minutes, the three studied Hardy's map, pointing to the main trail, Maddy's cabin, the creek where Alice and Mr. Hunt found Hardy, and so on. Alice stayed in the kitchen, cleaning up their abbreviated dinner but listening carefully to the discussion. The boy was greatly relieved that he had decided not to indicate anything on this big map about the cemetery yet. His plan, since its discovery, was to wait until he had found what he wanted and then make an impressive presentation to his mother—and now also to Lily Mae's great-grandmother. Yet it was beginning to dawn on him that he might not be able to keep this big secret as long as he had hoped.

"Okay, we had better get going, then." The older-looking officer stood up, followed by the other. "Your map is very helpful. If the attacker or attackers dealt with the young lady as they did with you, there is a good chance that she is in the vicinity." He looked at his partner. "We want you to come with us. You are a friend of the victim, and you might be able to identify clues."

Hardy smiled with relief, then looked over at his reliable, four-legged companion. "Can Rusty come, too? He knows the forest better than I do, and he brought my mom to me, all by himself."

The two officers looked at each other again. The older-looking one replied, "Sure, as long as he obeys you. Now, we will get some portable spotlights out of the squad cars, and a bullhorn." They walked out the front door to their vehicles. Alice followed Hardy into the laundry room, where he was rustling through the clothes for some outdoor wear. Grabbing his boots, he paused when he saw Alice.

"Honey, are you sure you feel well enough to go back out there tonight?"

"My head's stopped hurting, mostly." He spied his pack in the corner on the floor and decided it was better off up in his room. Grabbing one of its straps, he headed out the door to the stairs. "Besides, I can't sit here waiting for someone else to find Lily Mae!"

Alice grabbed his arm. "You be careful, and you do what the officers say. This is no time to try anything foolish!"

Hardy looked up and saw the plea in his mother's eyes. "I won't, Mama." He walked a bit stiffly up the stairs to his room and dressed for the search, while the officers returned to the cabin. Rusty barked and wagged his tail, sensing adventure. Hardy came down the stairs, ready to go.

"One more thing," the second officer said, looking at both mother and son. "By any chance, do you have an item of clothing or something that would have the young lady's scent on it? Perhaps your dog would be able to help us find her."

Hardy's face jumped. "Mom, where did you put Lily Mae's daypack?" Alice brought the pack out of the kitchen, then Hardy looked through it, pulling out her work gloves. He held them under Rusty's nose, and the dog began to sniff them all over. "Rusty, find Lily Mae. Where is Lily Mae?" Rusty sniffed some more, while Alice found a clean bag. They put the missing girl's gloves inside the bag, which Hardy then closed and stuffed into one of his coat pockets. Rusty was barking at the back door, when the two deputies and the slightly limping boy exited, with lights and bullhorn, following the dog, who ran to the trailhead and dropped his nose to the ground.

Alice closed the door and could hear Hardy's voice fading down the trail, "Rusty, where is Lily Mae?" She laid her head against the door and stood there quietly. After a few moments, her shoulders began to shake, and she could feel two warm rivulets moving down her cheeks. Drawing a long breath, she softly sobbed, leaning against the door, using the dish towel in her hand to wipe her nose.

Suddenly, the telephone was ringing. Alice turned and walked to the phone, wiping her eyes and taking another deep breath. "Hello? . . . Oh, Richard, I'm so glad to hear from you. Two deputies are out in the forest with Hardy and Rusty, looking for Lily Mae." She leaned back against the counter. "Well, I'm just feeling a bit overwhelmed at the moment . . . Yes?" She tipped her head forward, as if to hear the voice on the other end of the line more clearly. Time seemed to stand still. Then Alice sank, the counter catching her back, her free hand rushing to her forehead.

"Oh, Richard, tell me it's not true. Has anyone notified her next of kin? . . . When can you get back here? Lily Mae's mother and uncle are on their way . . . Okay . . . See you soon." Alice put the telephone back in its cradle and stood slightly bent over. Her lips quivered. She closed her eyes for a few moments, rubbing her forehead with the palm of her hand, deep in rumination. The light beams that darted across the walls did not get her attention, nor did the tire sounds on gravel in front of the house. At the knock on the door, Alice opened her eyes, put down the towel, sighed, and walked to the door.

"Mrs. Nolan! Mr. Clark! Please come in and sit down! The deputies and Hardy are out in the forest right now. Other officers are checking the roads for old pickups, and I just heard from Mr. Hunt. He had bad news about Maddy."

As THE SMALL SEARCH party made its way down the dark trail, lit with brilliant spotlights in an attempt to keep track of Rusty's whereabouts, Hardy couldn't remember if he had ever prayed this hard. When he was little, he used to pray for certain toys at Christmas and that God would bring him a daddy who lived with them and wasn't just in photographs. Now he was hoping that God would overlook those requests of self-interest and consider the scared boy's entreaties about his friends. He figured that these were reasonable petitions, since neither Lily Mae nor Maddy had done anything to deserve what happened to them. Yes, he was pretty sure that Maddy's defense of their cemetery investigation could be justified, even if she tried to take the pistol away from the man. Hardy remembered her saying during their dinner that a nephew brought her firewood. She called the man "Junior." Did he shoot her on purpose?

Rusty's barking got louder and faster, rousing Hardy from his anxious musings. He tried to spot the large, brownish-gray dog somewhere in the shadows. The officers stopped walking and shone the lights in the direction of the howling. One of the lights caught a glimpse of a small tuft of white scurrying a few feet off the ground and moving away from the search party. "Dog's scared up a deer," one of the officers intoned blandly. "Son, call the dog back and have him smell the gloves again."

The boy was glad to comply and had the bag with Lily Mae's gloves out for Rusty to sniff, when his four-legged companion returned to the trail. "Rusty, where is Lily Mae? Where is Lily Mae?" After some time with his snout in the bag, the dog wagged his tail and started trotting down the trail again. The search party of three, plus dog, was not talking, trying to move as quietly as possible, to be able to detect any sign of movement or sounds. There had not been time yet to travel as far down the trail as Hardy suggested they go, in order to reach the areas where he thought his friend might be. If the attacker's goal was to scare them both, and he left Hardy in the woods, then Lily Mae ought to be somewhere not far away. The attacker probably would have stayed away from the road, as it met Maddy's driveway below her cabin. He also probably would have taken her to a spot some distance from where Hardy ended up. In Hardy's mind, that left only two or three places. These were the search party's destinations.

He couldn't tell how long they had been gone. The darkness, the stillness, the cold air, the turns in the trail, and changes in elevation all left Hardy feeling that he was walking somewhere completely unfamiliar. He was very glad to have the one big map mostly done and in his possession. Even with the dark, the boy's handiwork was proving to be fairly accurate with distances and features. Having Rusty on the scent helped the boy, still hobbling a little, put his biggest fears in the back of his mind, at least for the time being.

Now they were arriving at one of the potential dump-off areas. Hardy got out the gloves one more time for Rusty, who sniffed them with gusto and then walked into the brush next to the trail. Deputies and boy followed, searchlights sweeping patterns across the ground. After ten minutes or so, the older-looking officer decided it was time to check one of the other locations. Hardy consulted his map and pointed them toward the one that was closest. Rusty walked ahead, as they made their way. About five minutes later, Rusty's nose leaned down into the trail path, and he started weaving excitedly back and forth.

Hardy saw what the dog was doing and whispered loudly, "Rusty, where is Lily Mae? Where is Lily Mae?" Sniffing as though he were inches from a fresh steak, Rusty moved left of the trail, into some light brush. Then he began to run in a crooked weave again and bark, sniffing every few seconds.

"Looks like he's got a fresh scent," the other officer said. "Let's go!" Keeping Hardy between them, the officers stepped into the brush, one with his beam aimed ahead at Rusty, the other sweeping either side of the direction of their movement. The shepherd mix was almost out of sight, now barking like he had treed a 'possum. Hardy started to run after him, but an officer grabbed his arm and put his other index finger up to his lips. Once again, the boy could feel his heart hammering in his chest, like it did earlier that day when he and Lily Mae were digging up Cherokee Ben's family headstones, like it did when he saw Maddy fall to the ground in front of her cabin, like it did when his unknown assailant grabbed him off the trail.

Besides Rusty's bark, Hardy thought he could begin to make out sounds like those he had heard earlier that night when he was thrown to the ground—gurgling, splashing sounds. It was another creek! Hardy knew which one, having drawn it out on his map. It couldn't be more than fifty yards away from where they were walking at the time. Then he realized that Rusty had stopped barking. Hardy was beside himself by then. "Lily Mae! Lily Mae!" He broke out from between the two officers and limped as fast as could toward the point at which he last saw Rusty. One of the officers kept a beam of light out ahead of him, as they followed. "Lily Mae! Lily Mae!" His head began to pound again, and he was short of breath already, but Hardy kept up his frenzied pace.

This creek was bigger than the one where Hardy had been thrown earlier, so it was no wonder that any other sounds made nearby it would not be easily heard from a distance. As he made his approach through the patchy, eerie light, Rusty's wagging tail was the first object that the winded boy could discern. He then made out Rusty's flank, and the dog's head faced in the opposite direction from which the boy was coming. It looked as though the dog was bending over something, but the spotlight beam did not reach that far. Frantically trying to get a better look, Hardy tripped and then had to painfully pick himself up off the damp, rocky ground. Rusty raised his head, barked a few more times, and moved just enough that Hardy, now only ten yards away, could see beyond the dog.

Lily Mae's head rested on the ground next to Rusty's paw, her jaw jerking at the heavy cloth wrapped through her mouth and tied tightly behind her head. Rusty bent over again to lick her face. "Lily Mae!" The dog moved aside, as Hardy rushed to kneel next to the girl, who was writhing and kicking the ground. "Lily Mae!" Hardy gasped to see her hands tied behind her back, her feet tied at the ankles, so that she could not get enough balance to sit up.

"Lily Mae! Let me get the gag out of your mouth!" The frightened girl still jerked and kicked. Hardy put his hand to the side of her face. "Lily Mae! It's me, Hardy." In the erratic light, he could see her turn to look up at him with one eye. He watched, as the terror in that eye disappeared and, a moment later, her body went limp. Hardy tried to untie the knot on the gag, but it had been cinched so tightly that it was too small for his fingers. He began to fumble around for his pocket knife, as the two officers arrived, led by the spotlights that now washed the entire scene almost as brightly as day. "Lily Mae, hold still for a moment!" With his knife's small blade, Hardy cut the gag off, as one officer did the same with her feet and the other for her hands.

"They took me! Dragged me away while I was nursin' Maddy! Tied me up and threw me here! And they slapped me, slapped me hard!" Now Hardy could see the swelling in Lily Mae's cheeks and some red marks on her face. He put his hand on her arm, and tears appeared in his eyes.

"But we found you! You're safe now!" The other officer had stood up and was sweeping the vicinity, with his spotlight and his pistol drawn, while the older-looking officer knelt next to Hardy and Lily Mae. "I got your gloves out of your pack, and Rusty sniffed 'em. That's how we found you as fast as we did!" As he spoke, the relieved boy saw Lily Mae beginning to shiver. The light jacket and jeans that she had donned for their daytime exploration were now nearly wet to the touch. The deputy produced a blanket that he had brought from the squad car. Hardy held her hand as Lily Mae slowly wobbled to her feet, then Hardy wrapped the blanket around her. She held the ends of it under her chin, until the shivering stopped. Looking at Hardy, she lowered her voice almost to a whisper and her eyes became glassy.

"Hardly, I was so scared! I thought they was gonna hurt me really bad!" All of a sudden, she noticed the bandage on her friend's temple. "What happened to you?"

"Somebody grabbed me when I was heading for the cabin. He threw me down by the other creek and kicked me in the head, and then he shot at Rusty!"

The older-looking officer shined a light on Lily Mae's face, checking for further injuries. He asked her to hold still, while he did a quick light-check for concussion. The girl, however, was regaining her composure quickly. "You seen Maddy?" she asked pleadingly.

"Mr. Hunt drove her to the hospital. I hope my mom has some news when we get back to our place."

"Young lady, you have been through quite an ordeal tonight. Do you feel strong enough to walk all the way back to the Newkirk's cabin?" The older-looking officer had a kind face.

Lily Mae scowled. "Jus' hungry. I can walk." Hardy rummaged through his coat pockets, until he pulled out a small candy bar in a worn wrapper. "Here, it's all I've got." She thanked him, unwrapped the candy bar, and took a bite.

"I don't see any signs of evidence here in this vicinity, although it's hard to tell at night. Let's get back to your house. My partner and I can radio into the station that we have found your friend." The older-looking officer gestured toward the trail with his spotlight, and the two tired youngsters began walking. Hardy knew it would take at least twenty minutes to make it back to the cabin.

Lily Mae finished the candy bar and leaned over to Hardy in the dim light. "You tell 'em about the . . . ?"

"No," the boy replied before she could finish her sentence. "Right now, they figure we got roughed up because we saw Maddy get shot." Lily Mae noticed that Hardy was limping. The deputies walked front and rear on the trail, still shining their lights on all sides, looking for clues.

"Your head hurt?" She looked at him the way she did at Maddy when they had dragged the old woman inside her cabin earlier that long day.

"A little. Mom made me take a pain-killer."

"What he say to you?"

"Somethin' about staying out of other people's business." Hardy paused. "Did they say anything to you?"

Lily Mae looked at the two sheriff's deputies before replying, then spoke in a whisper. "When they slap me, they say not to hang around with you no more, to stay away from here."

Hardy gulped and stared out into the darkness for a moment. "Then they must know that we found the cemetery. It must be about Cherokee Ben, but why?"

"Hardly?" She tugged a little on his coat. He turned toward her with a quizzical look. She lowered her voice again. "You see him?"

"You mean, the guy who grabbed me?" Hardy was not sure where her line of questioning was going.

"Yeah. What he have on?"

Hardy slowed down with the thought of the answer to her question. He whispered back, "I dunno for sure, but it seemed like he was covered with a big sheet or something."

Lily Mae squeezed Hardy's arm so quickly and firmly that he grunted in surprise. "Hardly, men who took me, they wore big sheets, too!" Then she paused and choked a little, as she barely whispered, "My mama tol' me about people like that."

Light from the back stoop of Rufus's cabin again shone unevenly down the last part of the trail. Long shadows reaching down the hill did not seem menacing now, like those in the thick of the forest had seemed earlier. The older-looking officer instructed his partner to accompany Hardy and Lily Mae into the house, while he went to his squad car to call in a report on the radio. Before they reached the back door, Alice flung it open, and two mothers rushed out to embrace their children, through sobs and tears. Mr. Hunt and Uncle James stood in the dining room, waiting their turn. Mrs. Nolan could not seem to stop embracing Lily Mae. "My baby! My baby! Praise the name of our sweet Jesus, my baby alive!" She touched Lily Mae's face and saw the red swelling on her cheeks. "They hurt you, child? They touch you?"

"I'm okay, Mama," her daughter replied, stoically. As if on cue, the men moved forward for greetings and embraces. Two or three conversations erupted at the same time, the youngsters trying to answer questions about their harrowing experiences, while both mothers kept asking Lily Mae if she was okay. The other officer was writing notes on a clipboard. In the middle of their well-meaning interrogation, Lily Mae finally asked, "How's Maddy?" No one heard her question, so she asked again, raising her voice. "How's Maddy?"

All conversation stopped. The youngsters looked at each other. Lily Mae asked yet again, "How's Maddy?" Her mother looked at Alice. She fiddled with her hands for a moment.

"Oh, honey, we wish we had good news. The doctors couldn't save her."

Chapter 13

Dead Ends

UNCLE RUFUS'S FUNERAL HAD been a lot different than Maddy's, Hardy was thinking to himself. His life had been celebrated at the Methodist church, near the courthouse in Pine Gap, where Rufus and his family, for who knew how many generations back, had been a part. The congregation was proud of its red brick building with stained-glass windows and maple pews, pipe organ, and paved parking lot off the street. On that day, the men had arrived wearing dress shirts and ties, and the women wore skirts and dresses. Hymns were sung from a hardbound hymnal, the pastor led a couple of prayers, church members read selections from the Bible, the pastor preached, and a few family members and friends talked fondly, and with gratitude, about Rufus. All in all, it was a rather quiet affair, lasting not much more than a half hour. After the service, everyone who could stay had eaten lunch in the church's fellowship hall.

Maddy's funeral was held at the Congregational Holiness Church, a few miles out of town on a winding county road. The old building was constructed of wood and had been painted white many years ago. A small cemetery lay to one side, and a packed-earth area in front served as a parking lot. An upright piano sat in one corner toward the front of the sanctuary—a space of modest size, with white paint on the walls and pine pews that had been purchased from another church in town when it remodeled. Maddy's relatives and friends arrived at the church scrubbed up from their outdoor chores—the men in clean plaid shirts and jeans, their hair slicked down and shiny, and the women in floral dresses with puffy sleeves, wearing their hair in buns. Hardy couldn't remember seeing any of these folks in town or at school events, although he wondered if one of the middle-aged men with a pot belly might have been Junior. Perhaps it was the one who seemed to be trying to look especially angelic, the boy with a shrinking, but sore, lump on his temple mused to himself.

Uncle James accompanied Lily Mae to the service. They sat in the back of the sanctuary on a bench and stayed there, even when Hardy had seen them come in and had waved at her to join them in the pew where he, Alice, and Mr. Hunt were sitting. A gray-haired, matronly woman played the piano for a few minutes before the hearse pulled up, and six men in dark suits lifted out Maddy's pine casket, set it on a metal frame with wheels, then walked solemnly beside the rolling ensemble, into the building and to the front of the sanctuary. As they moved up the center aisle, Hardy began to wonder if Junior was one of the dark-suited men. The boy hardly could imagine it!

Once the service began, he did not know any of the songs that were sung, but he hummed along as best as he could, watching his mother do the same. The preacher wore a wrinkled white shirt, a faded tie, and a sport coat with water or food stains here and there. A few minutes into his remarks, he got quite excited, Hardy thought, and occasionally spoke gibberish. Some of the people in the sanctuary started getting excited, too, swaying back and forth, waving their hands, looking up at the rafters, some of them yelling as the preacher got even more worked up. They must be pretty sad about Maddy's death, too, Hardy thought, and would miss her even more than he would. Alice and Mr. Hunt sat quietly throughout this animated episode, even when a young woman a few rows down jumped up screaming and then appeared to faint dead away in the side aisle, her eyes rolling around, head and hands twitching.

After all the clamor had subsided, the pianist played one more chorus that everyone sang or, if you were a visitor, mumbled. At that point, the six men in dark suits, who had been sitting on the first pew, took their positions around the casket and wheeled it back down the aisle. Piano music started again, as people rose from the pews and moved in an orderly manner toward either the back or side door. Lily Mae and Uncle James were waiting for Hardy's party at the back, and they walked out together, in time to see the same six men set Maddy's casket down next to an open grave on the far side of the cemetery. The small crowd assembled around it, standing on sections of green outdoor carpeting. Reading a few verses from the Bible, the now-hoarse preacher prayed another long prayer, punctuating it several times with an emphatic "Amen!" When he finished, the men in dark suits lowered the casket into the grave, using long ropes that they held and pulled out of the newly dug hole once the casket came to rest. A few older people picked up a handful of earth from the pile next to the grave and tossed it onto the casket. Everyone else walked away and began talking.

Alice and Mr. Hunt greeted Uncle James, while Hardy and Lily Mae stood uncomfortably next to each other. Without looking at his young companion, the boy mumbled under his breath, "Poor Maddy! She died tryin' to protect us!"

Lily Mae pretended not to hear him, even as she replied with a deadpan expression. "I stopped her bleedin', Hardly. She might o' been okay, if those men hadn't come!"

Hardy stuck his hands in his pockets and looked around as casually as he could manage. "Do you think they are here?"

"I can feel it!" Lily Mae replied. 'Member Maddy sayin' her nephew brought her firewood?"

"I remember." The boy was staring absently at the retreating funeral goers.

"Which one, you think?" She stared off in the other direction.

"I'm not sure. They all kinda look the same right now, maybe one of the pall bearers. Wouldn't that be something? Shoot your aunt, then act all goody-goody as you drop her in the ground!" Hardy was scowling by then and shaking his head.

"He's here, I know it! The other one, too. Tryin' ta see who been lookin' at me. Prob'ly thought we too scared to come!" Suddenly, she looked at Hardy intently. "Know what my mama say?"

He pretended that he still was ignoring her, but the heavy sigh that escaped his lungs right then was real. "I can guess."

"She say things too crazy for me an' you to do any more explorin' right now. Say one kidnappin' one too many. Next time be a lot worse." Lily Mae stopped talking as the two of them followed the adults slowly strolling back to their vehicles. Hardy's limp was just about gone. The emergency-room physician had checked over both youngsters and pronounced them shaken and bruised but otherwise in good condition. As Lily Mae turned to walk over to Uncle James's car, Hardy called to her, then looked around nervously.

"Maybe . . . uh . . . maybe we can talk on the phone once in a while. . . ." His voice trailed off when he saw her turn his way.

Hardy thought he could see a teary glisten in Lily Mae's eyes. She blinked several times before replying. "Yeah . . . that be okay . . . well . . . 'bye." Turning to open the passenger's side door of her uncle's vehicle, the tall girl ducked into the car before Hardy could see her sobbing. He walked faster, to catch up with Alice and Mr. Hunt, an uncomfortable lump quickly growing in his throat. The two teachers got into the front seat of Mr. Hunt's

car, and Hardy climbed into the back, putting his head in his hands and trying to hold still. The car was on the road before anyone spoke. Alice turned
around.

"Hardy, we were chatting with Lily Mae's Uncle James, and we agreed
to drive over to his house and talk over some things with Lily Mae and her
mother."

The boy leaned forward in the seat to look at his mother. "Is something
wrong? Is this about what happened to Lily Mae?" He was happy to get to
see her again so soon, but Alice's voice could not completely hide its ominous tone.

"Yes, and some other things, too. We'll talk when all of us are together."

Mr. Hunt drove his car back into town and then turned onto a street
leading to Lily Mae's neighborhood. The lanky girl and her uncle were getting out of his car when Mr. Hunt drove up to the curb. Everyone greeted
one another again and made their way into Uncle James's house, where Mrs.
Nolan was waiting for them. The dignified man invited his guests to sit at
the dining-room table. Hardy looked at Lily Mae. She raised her eyebrows
and shoulders back at him. Alice looked at both youngsters and then began
to speak.

"The two of you have had quite an adventure! All of us are very grateful
that neither one of you was seriously hurt, and we are deeply saddened that
Maddy was killed." She paused and took another breath. "We know that
you have enjoyed spending time out in the forest behind our cabin, being
outside and looking for little items from days gone by. It is a good pastime,
especially at your age. It helps you appreciate history and being part of this
community."

Alice looked around the table at all the adults assembled there before
continuing. "But things have changed since Maddy's shooting. You are no
longer safe out in the woods." She turned to face Mr. Hunt. "Richard?"

The history teacher stammered a little before speaking. "Kids, this is
an old town. There are families who have lived here for many generations,
and they know how things used to be. Some of them are not happy with
changes that come in our world, but some of these changes have to take
place, in order for our county to live up to the values that we claim in our
founding documents. Do you follow me?" Hardy and Lily Mae nodded.
Hardy's mouth felt dry.

Mr. Hunt cleared his throat and looked down at the table in front of
the two curious youngsters, choosing his words carefully. "There still are
folks living in this town and county who would be pleased if Lily Mae's family—and all the other families in this neighborhood—suddenly moved away.
There still are folks around here who took part in terrible crimes designed to

keep certain people from enjoying the same freedoms as others." He paused. "We believe that some of these folks are the ones who roughed you up in the forest. None of the old-timers will talk about it, but it's a good guess that they all know who did it."

Hardy couldn't keep quiet at this point. "So, are they gonna catch Junior and put him in jail for shooting Maddy?"

The adults all looked at each other with a mixture of surprise and resignation. Mr. Hunt replied. "The coroner has ruled Maddy's death a suicide."

"What?" The two explorers already had figured out that their wings were getting clipped, but letting Maddy's shooter go unnamed and scot-free rankled them both. "Suicide? We saw him do it! We can tell the sheriff our story. The deputies heard us!"

Uncle James answered Lily Mae. "Young lady, the powers that be have made their ruling and, for now, it will have to stand. It's not fair, but you know it's not the first time." He reached across the table and squeezed the upset girl's hand, as her mother put her arm on her brother's shoulder. "And I doubt it will be the last."

Hardy and Lily Mae looked at each other in pained disbelief. Before either one of them could think of something else to say, Alice continued. "Kids, we have been talking about what happened, and we are wondering if there is something else besides Maddy's shooting that would explain what happened to the two of you. Did something that Maddy said at dinner give you two ideas about secrets in the forest?"

Immediately, a shock went down Hardy's spine. His heart began thumping like a big drum, and the fading lump on his temple started throbbing again. Lily Mae was staring at him when he looked up. Alice directed her attention to the boy whose face was turning crimson. "Son?"

"Well," he began, "I was gonna tell you soon, but I wasn't quite finished." Suddenly, he had an idea. Looking at Lily Mae, he posed his mother a question. "Would it be alright if I tell you by talking to Lily Mae's great-grandmother?" The girl's eyes lit up.

Alice looked puzzled. "What do you mean?"

Hardy was getting excited. "You'll see! Can we . . . may we, please?"

Uncle James pushed his chair back from the table. She's in her room. I might have to wake her from a catnap, but the doctor says they make it hard for her to sleep at night." Tensions eased as Uncle James left the room, although the other adults were curious about what was to transpire. Moments later, Great-grandmother appeared in her wheelchair, which Uncle James guided to the end of the dining-room table. Her eyes lit up as she recognized both Lily Mae and Hardy.

"Children! Such a delight!" Lily Mae leaned over and kissed the old matriarch on the cheek. "And young Newkirk! You saved my little girl! How can I thank you?" The old woman's smile was warm and infectious.

Hardy protested with an embarrassed smile. "It was mostly my dog Rusty."

"A well-trained dog, he sounds." Her expression then changed, while her voice remained cordial. "Looks like our little secret plan led to big trouble! I am so sorry to hear about Maddy, very sorry. But you have somethin' to tell me, yes?" The old woman's sharp mind surprised Alice and Mr. Hunt, but everyone was waiting to hear what the youngsters had to say to her.

Hardy looked at Lily Mae. "You tell her."

"You sure?"

"Yeah! It's your story!"

Lily Mae took a deep breath, while everyone else at the table leaned forward a little. The girl smiled. "Great-gram, we found him! We found Cherokee Ben!"

As the other adults began looking at each other quizzically, Great-grandmother smiled knowingly. "And is he where we thought he be?" Heads were getting closer over the table top.

"In the cemetery, the one that Hardy found!" The boy shot a nervous glance at his mother who, upon hearing this totally unexpected announcement, cocked her head, pursed her lips, and squinted her eyes toward her son. Great-grandmother, however, deflected any other inquiries, at least for the moment.

"Then the old stories be true! Cherokee Ben had a child with a former slave."

Hardy had to jump in. "We found her grave, too, and a daughter . . . right next to Ben's!" For a few moments, he was able to relive the elation that was his and Lily Mae's that afternoon. "We made rubbings of all three headstones! That's what we were going to tell Maddy, when we saw the man with the firewood shoot her." Just as quickly, Hardy's elation plummeted, as his mind jarringly recalled images of her unconscious, bleeding body.

Great-grandmother reached out a hand and patted Hardy's. "Ya done what ya could, young Newkirk. It's all ya could do." The youngsters were wondering what would happen next. Mr. Hunt cleared his throat again.

"Well, this certainly is quite a revelation, to me, anyway, and I assume for the rest of us." He looked around the table, and the other facial expressions confirmed his comment. "As a history teacher, I get excited about discoveries like this. However, . . . " at this pause, Hardy was pretty sure he knew what was coming, "as one who knows more than I wish I knew about this town, you are playing with fire. Your lives were in danger once already. None of us wants anything else to happen to either one of you."

Hardy saw a knowing look on Lily Mae's face, and Alice could see Hardy's struggle to grasp what Mr. Hunt sought to convey. "Hardy, son," she began, "this incident was more than two kids riling up a couple of resentful men. Their actions show that you have uncovered something that this community is not ready to appreciate. In time, we hope they will. But, for now, talk of cemeteries and Cherokee Ben will have to stay between yourselves. It could become far too destructive otherwise."

As Alice stopped talking and settled back in her chair, Hardy was aware that the conversation was over. He looked over at Great-grandmother, who smiled at him and patted his hand once more. He turned to his husky-voiced companion, whom he had found bound and gagged by a creek in the dark of night. In that moment, she looked much wiser than he felt, and he was puzzled. "This means" he began, addressing no one in particular, "that we can't go in the woods or visit the cemetery anymore?"

"Not for the foreseeable future."

"Not even just Rusty and me?"

"Not even just Rusty and you."

"And we don't talk about the cemetery or Cherokee Ben with anyone?"

"Those stories stay in this room, among us."

Seeing Hardy's dejected expression, Lily Mae pointed at the boy's head. "'Member this goose egg, ya dodo?" He smiled, and the adults chuckled, relaxing a little.

Alice spoke again. "And, son, one more thing. We think it's best for a while that you and Lily Mae cool things at school . . . not hang around together."

The boy saw only one point for bargaining. "Can we talk on the phone?" His beseeching eyes worked the room.

Mrs. Nolan smiled. "Every day, but I'll have to set a timer!" Great-grandmother laughed heartily, followed by grins all around and certain red faces.

On the way home in Mr. Hunt's car, Hardy sat quietly in the back seat, while his mother talked school business with her fellow teacher. Images from the last week's events kept randomly appearing in his mind. Feelings of jubilation, horror, fear, and relief moved across his soul, as heartlessly as a cold winter wind. Only Rusty's barking from the top of the driveway shook the boy out of his jumbled reflections. He got out of the car to greet the loyal dog. As Mr. Hunt walked Alice to the door, Hardy overheard her say, "Thank you, Richard, for everything." The history teacher replied quietly and took her hand for a moment. Hardy had seen enough and walked with

Rusty around the back of the cabin. He was standing there, staring at the woodpile, Rusty licking his hand, when Alice opened the back door.

"Honey, how are you doin'?"

"Okay, I guess." He could hear her coming off the back step and walking toward him. She stood next to him. The boy sighed absently. "I miss the woods already."

"I can imagine. It's one of the reasons that I wanted to move here." She took a breath. "I guess we'll have to do some hiking around in other places . . . parks where dogs can walk on a leash."

"It's not the same." He didn't move or change his expression.

"No, nothing will be quite like it. Hopefully, some day you can go back out there and not worry about what others think. But, for now, it's best for everyone involved to stay away." She put her arm on his shoulder. He leaned away from her, just a little. "Honey, what's wrong?"

Hardy paused and spoke in a quiet voice. "I saw Mr. Hunt take your hand when you got out of the car."

Alice squeezed his shoulder. "Son, Mr. Hunt is a very fine man. I appreciate the energy he has given to help us during this difficult time."

"Yeah, I guess." He suddenly started walking to the back door. "I'm gonna change clothes and split some more wood." Alice watched him disappear into the house.

"Let me know when you get hungry, okay?"

Chapter 14

Rufus

HARDY'S THIRTEENTH BIRTHDAY CAME the week after Maddy's funeral. Alice arranged for a few of his school friends from Draper to drive up for the day. Hardy also invited a couple of boys whom he enjoyed from his Pine Gap classes, along with Lily Mae. Her mother decided that a birthday celebration would be safe enough, not drawing suspicion from anyone who still might be keeping an eye on the movements of the two teenagers. Rain that day answered the question of whether Hardy would have to make excuses for why they didn't hike in the woods, especially since he showed his guests some of the more interesting artifacts from his late-summer and early-fall explorations. None of those objects, however, even remotely hinted at the presence of a cemetery, nor did either of the young explorers breathe a word of the recent scare and tragic death.

For her part, Lily Mae displayed the same grace that impressed Hardy the night that Maddy came to dinner. Some of his Draper friends looked funny at each other when the quiet girl was introduced as Hardy's school friend, but by the end of the afternoon, no one seemed to care one way or the other. Hardy did blush a couple of times, upon hearing a good-natured tease of the adolescent, romantic kind. Lily Mae only smiled. Besides hamburgers and a vegetarian pizza (the latter being Hardy's concession to his mother), everyone feasted on a strawberry chocolate cake that Alice baked just for the occasion and ice cream from a local dairy. Hardy didn't even mind that Mr. Hunt was there to assist Alice in the kitchen. She was right, he admitted to himself, he really was a very nice guy.

Then came Thanksgiving. Alice invited Mr. Hunt to the family gathering in Draper. He volunteered to drive and invited Hardy to sit in the front seat. That way, they could talk while Alice rested in the back, after cooking until past midnight. It didn't take long for the conversation to turn to Cherokees, Moravians, and settlers. Hardy mostly asked questions, many of which Mr. Hunt could not answer, but they enjoyed talking, anyway. A couple of times, Mr. Hunt avoided Hardy's questions about Maddy and the white robes, and the boy eventually got the hint. Once the road signs mentioned Draper, Hardy talked about soccer, a game that Mr. Hunt had played and refereed.

School became both busy and festive, in the days before the long Christmas break. Teachers gave more tests and assigned reports with December deadlines. Basketball season began, and Hardy kind of wished that he had tried out after Halloween. Alice was busy with student art projects and a holiday art show of student works. The junior high school did not present a nativity play, but the band and choir performed a concert the Friday night before school recessed. Hardy decided that he wanted to sing in the choir next year, even though his voice was starting to sound like a foghorn sometimes. Since Maddy's death, he realized that he was making more friends at school. He and Lily Mae would wave at each other in the halls or classroom and talk on the phone for a few minutes most days around dinnertime.

Still, when he crawled into bed at night and the amateur adventurer closed his eyes, all that Hardy could see was the forest—pines, oaks, and poplars spread across the hills and hollers. All he could smell was the fresh scent of the outdoors and smoke curling through the air from Maddy's cabin. All he could hear were the woodpeckers, the thrashers, and the burbling of the creeks, rushing fast, dancing over smooth stones following a hard rain. All he could think about was the cemetery and Cherokee Ben.

Now that the holiday vacation had begun, Alice reminded Hardy of things to get ready for Christmas. Alice had invited their family up to the cabin, on the promise of "a good chance for snow!" This meant that company would be arriving mid-morning and staying all day. He and Alice would attend the Christmas Eve service at the Methodist church and, then, get home to complete their preparations. Alice gave him a list of his responsibilities, including deadlines for each one. The wrapping of family gifts was on his list and, fortunately, it was not "due" until the twenty-fourth.

Cleaning, vacuuming, washing, cleaning, polishing, splitting, stacking, shopping, cleaning—Hardy stayed quite busy in and around the house, getting ready for Christmas, so he pretty much had forgotten about Uncle Rufus's journal. It had been put somewhere but had not surfaced since unpacking from the move. Alice asked him to make a few small wooden toys for the young cousins, and Hardy was glad to do it. He drew out a few figures and decided how he would construct them. A visit around the woodshed produced the necessary raw materials. The cutting, carving, and fitting took place in the laundry room. When he finished, he took them up to his room and sat them on his dresser.

Hardy woke up on Christmas Eve day, wondering what he would get for Christmas. Alice needed his help in the kitchen with the pies and such, which distracted his mind a little bit. She let him call Lily Mae for a few minutes, and the two traded schedule information for the upcoming couple of days. He promised to call her the day after Christmas and hung up. Rain was forecast into the evening. The boy was feeling a little restless.

Services for Christmas Eve were held early in the evening. That way, families with young children could have time for festivities and still get kids into bed at a decent hour. The sanctuary at the Methodist church was full. It had been hard to find a parking space in the lot. The choir sounded majestic, the pastor gave out little brass bells made in Bethlehem to all the young children, and the story of Jesus's birth was presented with solemn simplicity. Hardy looked around and recognized a number of adults and kids his age there. As Alice drove the car back to the cabin, Hardy was starting to feel at home in the mountains.

Alice put a Christmas album on the record player when they got inside. She then returned to the kitchen, while Hardy went up to his room to wrap gifts. He left the door open in order to hear the music gliding up the staircase. Gathering up the articles and boxes to be wrapped, he organized them against one wall and laid the wrapping paper, scissors, ribbon, and tape next to the side of his bed. Then he sat down in the middle of the floor, to begin his final task.

Alice had turned over the record on the stereo, when Hardy was finishing the third or fourth wrapping. There were several more to finish, but the boy had nothing else to do, and he was starting to get sleepy anyway. Rusty was curled up in a funny place near the head of his bed, taking it easy, while still calmly watching his master's activity. One of the items to be wrapped was oddly shaped and would not fit into any empty boxes, so Hardy used up some of what was left of his evening energy figuring out how to make it look nice. A few cardboard pieces and extra strips of tape finally did the trick, and Hardy was pleased with the attractive outcome. He held up the finished product as though on display, announcing to no one in particular, "Ta-da!"

Rusty raised his head and wagged his tail, which at that moment was hidden under the front of the bed. As he wagged, his master heard a peculiar "thump" and, curious at the sound, bent down to take a look. Rusty wagged again, thinking that Hardy was approaching him to scratch his chin. With his head almost at floor level, the boy could tell that Rusty's tail was hitting against a smaller-sized cardboard box. Flattening out on his stomach, Hardy reached under his bed to pull out the box and see what it was. As he pulled it toward him, another "thump," this one barely audible, came from behind the box. Hardy got out the box, from under the bed, and stuck his hand back into the dark space. Something else was there, a little smaller and much flatter than the box. He had his hand on the object and was pulling it toward the edge of the bed, when he suddenly realized what it was.

Still lying on his stomach, Hardy turned the object over to hold it in both hands and gasped. About nine inches long and seven inches wide, covered with leather, the roughly rectangular item looked weathered by time. One side of the long end consisted of book binding with a stiff spine. On the opposite end, smooth edges—an inch or more thick—of writing paper were visible. Hardy quickly opened the pages to the front leaf. "Rusty!" he exclaimed, then immediately dropped his voice. "Rusty! It's Uncle Rufus's journal!"

Jumping up to close his bedroom door, Hardy then sat against the side of his bed and began thumbing through the pages of this unanticipated discovery. His fingers trembled as he skimmed the handwritten text for something that would catch his eye. He flipped back to the first few pages, thinking that perhaps he missed something during his initial moments of excitement. Suddenly he froze, staring in disbelief at the top of one page, unable to speak. His eyes darted back and forth, reading the same few lines over and over, as if he could not comprehend them. Then the book dropped in his lap, his head fell back against the bed, and Hardy uttered in a low voice, "Hoe-lee cow!"

For a minute or so, Hardy sat on the floor, his eyes closed, while the Christmas music from the living room continued to drift softly up to the landing. Slowly, he opened his eyes and exhaled, looking around the floor at the rest of the gift-wrapping to finish. Picking up one of the toys, Hardy reached for some paper with bells on it and began sizing a cut. "Rusty," the boy spoke under his breath, "I have something I have to do tomorrow, but you have to stay here."

When all the wrapping was finished, Hardy carried the packages downstairs and put them under the pine tree that he had cut—the one that had been growing by the other side of the woodshed. He checked with Alice about any last-minute chores, and she asked him to move the china to the dining-room table. That done, the boy picked up some things in the laundry room, forced a yawn, told his mother he was heading for bed, and said good night. "I'll see you Christmas morning, son!" Alice smiled as his footsteps echoed off the stairway treads.

An hour before dawn, Hardy crawled out of bed as quietly as he could and turned on the lamp next to his bed. In the opposite corner of the room, he had laid his outdoor clothes and boots that he had retrieved from the laundry room the night before. Once dressed, the sleepy boy found his day-pack in the closet and checked the flashlight, trowel, maps, waxed paper, crayons, and other supplies that he and Lily Mae had been using. He slung the pack over his coat and slipped his arms through the shoulder straps. Then, opening his bedroom door as slowly and quietly as possible, Hardy stepped gingerly down the stairs. Rusty was up and wagging his tail at the bottom of the steps. Hardy bent over and whispered in his ear, and the big dog went back to his warm spot by the fire. Tiptoeing to the back door, Hardy lifted the spare door key from its hook, unlocked the door, opened it, stepped outside, eased the door closed, and locked it with the key.

Turning away from the cabin, the determined young teen on a mission of stealth was greeted by the dark gray that teases before dawn. The only sound he could hear, as he walked softly to the trailhead, was the dripping of dew and late-night rain off the roof and trees. Once at the trail, Hardy turned on the flashlight and began to jog, as fast as the light would allow, down the first big hill, around a bend, back around another bend, up a draw, past a clearing on one side and overgrown brush on the other, near the creek where he had been thrown down, and climbing another high spot. Hardy was huffing after a few minutes but determined to keep his pace.

Trusting that he knew these woods well enough not to consult his maps in the dark, Hardy was grateful to see that the dark, gray sky was slowly becoming brighter. A few twinges in his foot and occasional throbbing in his head reminded him of that day, and he wondered if this was such a good idea. But surely, he reasoned, no one would be out in these woods this early on Christmas morning!

Before much longer, Hardy turned onto the last leg of his dawn-light mission, but he had to slow down. The terrain here challenged him enough in daylight. His heart was racing in part, however, because the destination now loomed near, and he was making good time. Glad that he wore gloves, and realizing that, in his haste, he had left his walking stick in the cabin, the boy grabbed a sturdy, fallen limb to help with his balance. The climb was getting steeper, but Hardy knew that a flat spot was near, signaling the end of his journey. Perspiration cooled the band around his hat, as he grunted a couple more times and pulled himself up to where he could get at least a dim look at his destination.

Dark gray lingered lazily as the sky visible through the trees ahead of him was gently turning to a pale white. Hardy estimated that he still had time to get back to the cabin before his mother woke up. Standing up straight, shaking off the tension of this fast-paced expedition, the boy who had thrown danger to the wind then turned to get his first look. He squinted into the dim shadows arching overhead but walked forward confidently, getting his bearings with familiar reference points. Something looked a little different here, Hardy thought, but it still was too dark to know for sure.

"Over there," he thought, "is where I remember them." Taking several more steps in that direction, Hardy felt puzzled again by a sensation that something had changed. Stopping momentarily, he looked ahead about thirty feet and was sure that he could make out the hub of his target location.

Yes, there it was! Ben's headstone, just as he recalled it from that day. He was here to find one more, just one for now. Then he remembered his flashlight again and pulled it out of the coat pocket. He aimed the beam at Ben's stone, then wife Abigail's, then daughter Charity's. When he moved the flashlight beam again, he suddenly realized what was different. Backing up several feet, Hardy swept the flashlight beam around him, looking at sections of the cemetery on which he and Lily Mae had worked. He blinked his eyes. "What?" He blinked them again.

Everywhere Hardy looked, he could see headstones. Across the space where he and Lily Mae had worked, there were several more headstones cleared off. Even in the sections where they had not done any digging, headstones were visible. Whether flat or upright, all were cleared off and clean, almost shiny like new. As he walked around the entire cemetery, Hardy shook his head. "I don't get it! What happened? None of these had the earth dug away from them when we were up here!" He was talking only to himself, as if to check his sanity.

Then it hit him. "Hey, that means . . . !" He turned back and ran over to Ben's headstone, as the beam of the flashlight was almost blending into the light of dawn. Frantically glancing to the right and left for what seemed like hours, Hardy suddenly stopped and shouted, "There it is!" He pulled off the pack, removed a piece of clean wax paper, rummaged in a small pocket for a dark-colored crayon, and began carefully rubbing the newly discovered stone. As quickly as he dared, he finished the task and put everything away. Slinging the pack over one shoulder, the elated boy ran to the edge of the cemetery and then stopped, turning around for a final look. Now, as unforeseen as just about anything that Hardy could have imagined, there it was, something that he had thought he might never have a chance to gaze upon, the graves of this historic cemetery, each one cleaned up for the world to see, fully legible again, not abandoned, not forgotten, not to be disgraced.

Hoping that Alice would still be asleep, Hardy clambered down the small, partially hidden bluff and to the trail, setting a jogging pace that he thought would get him home in less than ten minutes. His mind filling with wonderful, new thoughts, he hardly paid attention to his feet. He was so excited that he could have yelled at the top of his lungs all the way back. The flashlight was not necessary much of the time now, except to keep him focused on the trail. When he saw the last stretch up ahead, Hardy slowed down to a quick walk, hoping that he could breathe easily enough to talk when he got home. Another minute and he was striding toward the back door.

With the key in his hand, the sweating, exuberant boy turned the lock and quietly stepped into the cabin. He closed the door delicately and stood still for several seconds. Good, he thought to himself, Alice must still be sleeping. The pack came off and was set by the counter as Hardy tiptoed to the telephone, greeted by a wagging Rusty. He dialed a number and waited until a voice on the other end of the line answered. Almost whispering, Hardy spoke into the phone. "Hello, Mrs. Nolan? Please excuse me for calling this early. . . . Merry Christmas to you, too! . . . May I speak with Lily Mae, please? I have some news that I know she will want to hear!"

"Hardy Newkirk, what in the world are you doing up this early on Christmas morning? Why do you have your coat and boots on?" Alice was standing at the other end of the room, wrapped in her housecoat, hair going every which way, eyes squinting, but having no problem mustering a parental tone of disapproval.

Grinning with anticipation of his conversation with Lily Mae, Hardy whirled around. "Uh, Merry Christmas, Mom! I have something to . . . Oh, hi, Lily Mae! Merry Christmas! . . . Yeah, I know it's early, but guess what? We're cousins! . . . Cousins! . . . You and me . . . we're cousins! I found Uncle Rufus's journal last night." At this statement, Hardy looked over at his mother, her arms folded, waiting to make sense out of her son's behavior. "Yeah, it was stuck under my bed, out of sight. Anyway, I was reading through it, and I found a part where Rufus tells where his name came from. Guess who he was named after? . . . How'd you know that? . . . You sure, or did you make a good guess?"

"Anyway, I had to find out if Rufus was right, so I got up early this morning and ran to the cemetery, and there it was! There is another headstone near Ben's, and it says, "Rufus Clark, son." My uncle was named after Cherokee Ben's son!" By this time, Alice was standing next to Hardy, captivated by the story that he was telling Lily Mae. "And you won't believe this part! Somebody cleaned up the whole cemetery! . . . I'm not kidding! Every headstone has been cleaned off and polished up! It looks like a real cemetery now! . . . No, I didn't read any more of them. I wanted to get back and call you right away!"

"Anyway, that means we're cousins! You and me, we're cousins! Isn't that something? Nobody can take that away from us! Be sure to tell your great-grandmother, too! . . . Well, I'd better hang up now. We'll talk again, maybe tomorrow; okay, cousin? . . . 'Bye, . . . and Merry Christmas again!"

Hardy hung up the telephone and blew out a big breath of air. Alice scratched her head. "Well, well, that was a Christmas present no one saw coming! What did Lily Mae say when you told her?"

"She said she likes knowing for sure that I am not only her friend, but we are kinfolk, too." Hardy paused, thinking for a second or two. "She also said that she knew for a long time. She said she could feel it." He leaned against the counter, and Alice put her hand on his shoulder, noticing for the first time that her son was as tall as she. He pursed his lips, "How did she know?"

Alice smiled. "There are ways of knowing that don't depend on uncovering gravestones or reading journals. What you have done frightens people who don't want to know the world as it really is. Someday, maybe that fear will go away. In the meantime, I hope you will cherish your friendship with Lily Mae. It is all too rare."

Hardy had been staring at the counter, listening carefully to his mother, but he wasn't sure if he understood everything she said. Looking at her warm face, he asked innocently, "So, when can she and I go exploring again? There's a lot more to discover out there!"

Alice paused for a moment, glancing absently into the living room, then tossed her head toward the back door. "Come with me," she said, in a tone of voice that both bewildered and intrigued her son. She walked to the door and opened it while pulling her housecoat tighter around her body. Rusty reached the door before Hardy did, but Alice politely shooed him away. She stepped out on the porch as Hardy joined her.

Dew dripped, almost like rain, off the back stoop. The tree line facing them blocked most of the north sky, but daylight glistened light-orange hues off the wet, bare branches and pine boughs. Alice put one arm around Hardy's waist and gave him a squeeze, the kind he remembered as far back as his memory could muster. They stood still, watching the trees slowly change color as water drops plunked on the soggy ground in front of them.

"You love it out here, don't you?"

Still glowing inside from his early-morning discovery, the boy smiled as he stared out at the young day. "Yeah, I really do."

Alice had not moved. "Uncle Rufus used to say, 'If you want to fly with the doves, you'd better learn how the snakes crawl!'"

His eyes darting back and forth at nothing in particular, Hardy squinched up his face. "What does that mean?"

Alice smiled and turned her head in his direction, as if to relish her son's moment of pause. "I think," she replied deliberately, "that Uncle Rufus would want you to figure that out on your own."

Hardy studied the damp ground in front of him, and then exhaled. Turning to his mother, he mused, "Uncle Rufus was a wise man, wasn't he?"

Still smiling, Alice put her hand on the back of Hardy's neck. "Rufus was a very wise man, and I hope that you will grow up to be one, too."

Just then, Rusty started to bark from inside the kitchen door, so mother and son turned around and went back into the cabin.

The old stories keep whispering, until no one listens for them anymore.